CIRCLING EDEN

*A Novel of Israel
in Stories*

CAROL MAGUN

Academy
Chicago
Publishers

Published in 1995 by
Academy Chicago Publishers
363 West Erie Street
Chicago, Illinois 60610

Printed and bound in the U.S.A.

Library of Congress Cataloging-in-Publication Data

Magun, Carol, 1949–
    Circling Eden : a novel of Israel / Carol Magun.
        p.   cm.
    ISBN 0-89733-412-4 : $19.95
    1. Israel-Arab War, 1973--Fiction.   I. Title.
PS3563.A3515C57 1994
813'.54--dc20   94-37513
                                                          CIP

CONTENTS

I t takes so little, so infinitely little, for a person to cross the border beyond which everything loses meaning: love, convictions, faith, history. Human life – and herein lies its secret – takes place in the immediate proximity of that border, even in direct contact with it; it is not miles away, but a fraction of an inch.

Milan Kundera
The Book of Laughter and Forgetting

For Moti, Koby, Ariella

CIRCLING EDEN

1.
MAKE-BELIEVE

R ebecca jiggled the key in the lock, pushing
hard, down a bit, to the side, up again. Nothing worked. She closed her eyes, didn't care
if the door opened or not, but the lock wasn't
fooled. *"Lech le'azazel!"* Go to Hell! Lately it seemed
that this was to be the extent of her Hebrew conversation. She kicked the door and headed around to
the side of the house and her bedroom window.

She climbed up onto the upside-down clay
planter, always ready beneath her window, and
swung open the green iron shutters. The telephone
was still ringing. She knew it was Ethan. A rabbi's
son from Las Vegas, he had tutored her for this
morning's Hebrew final, the one that would decide
whether she'd be stuck in the English section for
visiting Americans or be allowed to take courses in
"easy Hebrew" at the university. He was also the

closest thing she had over here to a girlfriend, and she looked forward more to their kibbitzing, as he called their daily telephone conversations, than their occasional lovemaking.

And then, just as she pushed the window open and hoisted herself up over the sill, the ringing stopped. She tumbled headlong onto her bed. But something was wrong, she realized, and almost as she thought it, someone pinned her arms high behind her back.

"*Haamerika'it.*" More groan than word. Then the weight on top of her went suddenly limp.

She recognized the smell of his body even before she noticed the uniform in a heap on the floor, dusty boots still in the pantlegs. "Yigal." She tried to catch her breath. "Yigal." For almost two months now they had been sharing the same bed, he on weekends, she during the week, but they had never met. That was the arrangement Rebecca had worked out with Mrs Lipski: Rebecca could have the room on the condition that she turn it over to the widow's son on Shabbat when he was expected home from the army. "Nice to meet you," Rebecca said in her best three-month-old Hebrew.

By the time she gathered herself up, he was leaning against the headboard, bare to the waist, a sheet wrapped tight around his middle. He had a frowning, unshaved face and red watery eyes, not at all what his photograph had led her to expect.

She tried to ask him what he was doing here on a Tuesday, but again the Hebrew phrases refused to come. Just like this morning.

"Americans don't use doors anymore?" he exploded in English.

"My key doesn't always work. And never when I'm in a hurry." Her initial impulse had been to clear out, hand the bed over to him, but his arrogance changed her mind. After all, it was Tuesday, her day for the bed. She tucked her legs under her and faced him across the length of the mattress.

Yigal squinted, holding his arm up against the white light that flooded in through the now-open shutter. "You don't look like you're in a hurry," he said very seriously.

She tossed her hand in a typically Israeli gesture. She had more luck with the gestures than the language. "The phone was ringing. It stopped."

"The phone?" He broke into a grin. "And who you want to call you?"

She hesitated. For the first time she recognized him from the picture she had found tucked between the pages of his English grammar book. It was a glossy black-and-white army photograph, and he was decked out in full battle gear. Only his chin strap flapped open, his helmet sat crooked on his head, a jaunty smile took up most of his face. He looked more like a good-natured kid on a hike than the commando she'd imagined from his mother's talk. One day she even showed the picture to Mrs Lipski, just to make sure the boy really was Yigal, and not some cousin or friend. Mrs Lipski, faded and stringy, stared at the picture a long time.

"It's not real," she said at last, jerking her head in what Rebecca had come to realize was a nervous tic.

Rebecca peered at the upside-down soldier. "The smile?"

"The battle. All make-believe. Your Mickey Mouse."

"Oh." She had difficulty understanding Mrs Lipski. Those first weeks she had blamed the woman's staccato English, more pellets than phrases. She was never quite sure how to string them together. But lately she noticed that Mrs Lipski seemed to be watching *her* lips, as if she were having the same problem following Rebecca.

Mrs Lipski strained forward. Her crepe skin formed a rift from forehead to chin. "Can it be? The Golani? You never heard?"

Rebecca started chewing her lip.

"It's our Oxford and Cambridge," Mrs Lipski continued, her voice falling to a confiding whisper.

"Only no fancy degrees. You pass the big test, you get a pin. An eagle with claws. Over here." She touched her flattish bosom. "You understand?"

"Kind of."

Mrs Lipski pulled back with an exasperated sigh. "The test, the battle," she said, shaking her finger back and forth. "Not real bullets."

"Oh. . ." Rebecca stopped chewing her lip. "You mean the test is a mock battle."

"Mock? Is funny, no? Yes, Yigal's happy. He passed. Me?" Mrs Lipski pressed her palms together and brought them to her chin. "God no pass him." Then, without another glance at the picture, she handed it back, as if it were really Rebecca's, and turned away.

Rebecca returned the photograph to the English grammar, but instead of putting the book back on the shelf, she kept it on the nightstand beside the bed. She liked to read the Hebrew words scribbled in pencil next to the English, the translated idioms. "A rolling stone gathers no moss." She remembered learning that one in French. But it was the picture of the boy, the smile, she somehow always came back to.

"So who you want to call you?" Yigal repeated, still grinning.

"No one in particular," she said with a shrug. "I just know that if it rings during the day, with your mother at work, it's for me."

"And for that you jump through a window?" He shook his head.

The sheet around his middle had loosened and Rebecca noticed dark curls sprouting from the smooth skin. She looked away. Remembering the pin Mrs Lipski had mentioned, she studied the uniform on the floor, first the pocket, then the shoulder, but she could see no pin or patch or rank anywhere. Only the word, Zahal, the Hebrew abbreviation for the Israel Defense Forces, stamped in faded black letters. "They're battle fatigues," she whispered, turning back to him.

He said nothing, just stared.

Finally, she understood. He'd been out on a commando raid the night before and was now home on leave. He must have just thrown himself on the bed to sleep. Her chest contracted, with shame, selfishness, her own stupidity. She was about to apologize for disturbing him, but even in English her words were suddenly slow in forming and he got there first.

". . . I'm sorry if I hurt you, I didn't mean to," he mumbled, looking at his hand, massaging it. "I was just dozing off and. . ."

"And you thought it was still last night."

He jerked his head, almost like his mother. "I forgot the *amerika'im* love the psychiatry. Shrinks, they call the *psychiatrim*, no? In the army magazine I read about an *amerika'it* who even sent her dog to a shrink."

She flushed. "Listen. It's Tuesday. My day for the bed." She swung her hand toward the door. "You can sleep in your mother's bed."

"I don't want to sleep in my mother's bed." He reached across and caught her above the elbow. "I want to sleep in my bed. With you."

She pulled her arm free. "Is that also what they tell you in your army magazine? An *amerika'it* will sleep with anyone?"

"Why you have the birth control pills?"

"Why do you go through my things? You have no right." And it wasn't just her pill dispenser he'd examined, spinning the round plastic cover like a broken telephone dial so that the dates were all wrong. For weeks now she'd found letters from Michael folded against the crease, snapshots out of order, even her passport upside down in her travel wallet. Not that his curiosity about her had really bothered her. Just the opposite. Saturday nights first thing she'd do was go through her possessions, one by one, determining what he had touched, speculating what he might have thought.

He smiled, and she blushed deeper. She knew what was coming.

"You read my books. You sleep in my bed." He bunched up the sheet, her sheet, in his right hand.

"And you could at least change the sheets," she countered, fighting the urge to yank it from his hand. For the first couple of weeks, she had changed them herself, refusing to complain. She couldn't bear to justify Mrs Lipski's view of her as a spoiled *amerika'it*. Then, the third week, she had been so tired after having spent Shabbat on the beach with Ethan that she crawled straight into Yigal's unmade bed. Since then their shared sheets never bothered her.

"In the army I must to sleep on my ammunition. I hate the smell." He hesitated, grinning, almost sheepishly. "A woman's smell is much nicer."

"Yes. I guess it is," she said. Then she could think of nothing else to say.

After a silence he held out his hand.

This time she reached back.

Afterward, Rebecca felt the hot sun through the window, the sweat on Yigal's back, and knew it was for Yigal that she had come here, to this country, this house, this bed. Since high school, she had assumed that she would spend her junior year in Paris — all part of a no-nonsense plan that led from college, through law school, to a partnership in her father's firm. She had no brothers, and her father had raised her to outrun, outsmart, outfinagel any guy. And she had. Then one day in her sophomore year, she was lying in bed with Michael in his room at Yale when the news came on. At the end there was an interview with some Jewish teenagers who had gone over to Israel a few years back, just after the Six Day War. Against a backdrop of date palms they talked about what it was like, what they were doing, why they had stayed. Suddenly, Michael reached over and flicked off the switch. She turned it back on.

"Afterwards," she said, brushing his hand from her breast.

Michael sat up and reached for his underwear. "No thanks."

"Don't get so pissed," she said, not bothering to even look at him. "It's almost over."

"For chrissakes you're not even Jewish."

"There. Over." She turned off the television and nestled back into the pillow. She had a great body and liked showing it off. "Of course I'm Jewish," she said, only now really registering what he'd said. "You know that." How could he not know? They had been lovers for over a year. She had told him things she had told no one else.

He shook his head.

"For chrissakes my name's Rebecca."

"Rebecca Harrison," he smiled back. "Hey, it's no big deal. I guess it just never came up." His underpants were off again, and he was reaching for her.

"My grandfather changed. . ."

"It's not important," he said, stopping her words with a kiss.

But as soon as they finished making love, she started in again. "But I must have told you about my grandfather, how he'd take me behind his store, to the old warehouse, and show me this peddler's cart that had belonged to his father, my great-grandfather. . . "

"Becky, what's the point?"

There was a silence.

"I don't know," she finally said. "But I feel as if I just discovered I shrank an inch, or my IQ dropped ten points. Or I couldn't remember the opening stanza to Longfellow's 'Evangeline.' You know, 'This is the forest primeval. . . '" She looked over at him. "Or are you going to tell me I never told you that either?"

"Yes, I know all about your 'Evangeline,'" he sighed. "You used to recite pages and pages of it in

the woods behind your house. You were seven. . . ."
"Six."

She applied to the junior-year program in Jerusalem without telling a soul, not Michael, not her parents, not even her college advisor. She feared she would be expected to provide answers, reasons, explanations. And she had none. Just the vague presentiment that there might be less of her than she'd always assumed. To her surprise, when she finally announced that she would be spending the following year in Jerusalem, not Paris, no one asked, no one probed, no one challenged. Instead, they ascribed to her all sorts of reasonable motives she might have had but didn't. To her father it was a cut-and-dry case of "flirtation with Zionism"— not so different, he insisted, from his own "adolescent flirtation with Communism" in the thirties. A mistake, no doubt, but one she probably had to get out of her system. "Like a bug, a virus." Michael, much more laid back, just called it her "Jewish thing" and gave her a plastic figurine of a soldier with a red-and-white striped parachute as a going-away present.

At the airport everyone seemed to know one another already. They hugged hello. They exchanged news of teachers and camps and friends.

They compared lists of what they'd brought. Hair conditioner, Tampax, toilet paper, erasable typing paper, peanut butter, tuna fish. Apart from her clothes, Rebecca had brought only a set of sheets, a sleeping bag, a pocket sewing kit (her mother's idea) and a Swiss army knife (her father's).

"Israel is a land of many immigrants. Israel is a land of many climates. Israel is a land of many borders. . . "

The group leader shouted to make himself heard over the non-stop chatter, still going strong after almost twenty hours of travel. NIFTY. NEFTY. BEFTY. By the time the bus deposited them outside the boxy highrise dormitory at the edge of Jerusalem, the words sounded less like acronyms for Jewish youth groups than secret passwords between members of one huge club. Rebecca didn't even know the Hebrew alphabet. For her first month she believed the poster on the back of the Egged bus advertised "Lugum" soda in English, not Tempo soda in modern Hebrew script.

Only Ethan found her ignorance touching. "How did a nice girl like you end up in a place like this?" They were trekking across the wadi from the bus stop to the university. It hadn't rained since spring, and everything that should have been green was brown. Her eyelids burned. The blisters on her feet

— 20 —

were coated with dust.

"'This is the garden primeval. . . '" she managed to get out before she choked up.

An hour later she was in the central post office, on the phone to her father. "The virus is gone. I'm better. I want to come home."

He laughed, a bad sign. He never gave in to her when he laughed. "Oh no, sweetheart," he finally said. "You made your bed. Now you sleep in it. It won't kill you."

"How do you know? You should see the Americans they stuck me with."

"Then move."

She moved to the Lipskis.

The room had been listed with the student housing agency, but when Rebecca called, the woman insisted that the room was not for an *amerika'it*. Rebecca showed up anyway.

The house itself was one of the oldest outside the Old City walls. Once grand, it was now dilapidated and cut up into three flats. Laundry flapped from rusted balconies. Succulents sprouted from cracks in the foundation. Even the garden had gone to seed, palms mixed with pines and sedgy grass, no flowers at all. But the sunken pool was still filled with water and stocked with the largest goldfish Rebecca had ever seen. The woman—no hips, fair, hair drooping into a sloppy bun — took her first into the bathroom. "No heat, no running hot water, and the tub . . . kaput." Rebecca noticed only the scrolled ceramic tiles hanging loose on the wall.

The woman then took her to the bedroom, next to the bathroom and half the size. "The servant's room. Many years ago." It reminded Rebecca of a monk's cell, except for the white light that streamed in from the single window.

"I'll take it."

"Impossible. Not for an *amerika'it*."

"But I'm not *really* an *amerika'it*," Rebecca pleaded.

"My older son comes home on Shabbat. The room is for an Israeli student who also goes home."

"I'll leave for Shabbat," Rebecca interrupted, without even considering where she'd go.

Mrs Lipski hesitated, then broke into a crooked smile. "My goldfish, you want to see?"

Rebecca closed her eyes, aware now only of Yigal's body, covering her, weighing her down with pleasure. She suddenly knew what had been bothering her these past months: a growing sense of lightness, of floating past people and things. Untouched and not touching.

She heard the telephone ring, but paid no attention, until Yigal shifted his weight onto his knees.

"Your telephone," he said.

"So what?"

She tried to draw him back to her, but he ducked her embrace and sat up.

"You going to pick up, or I?"

"Please don't. . ." she murmured, but he was already on his way out the door.

"She moved," she heard Yigal say, first in English, then in Hebrew, before he banged down the receiver.

Back in the room, she watched him pull on his clothes. "He doesn't mean anything to me," she said, breaking the silence.

"Not important. In the army we, too, are used to the fucking. People come together, for an hour, a night, and don't see each other again."

"That's not what I meant. I meant he's just a friend."

Yigal glanced over. "I meant you and me."

She winced. "Speak for yourself. I feel as if I've known you for months. Ever since I moved here."

"My mother said she don't want to give you the room, but you don't listen. You never listen."

"What else does your mother say?"

"You buy bread, and let it get hard as stone. Your milk, it goes sour before you open it. Your friend, she can't tell if it's a boy or a girl. And in the garden you take off your top and don't care who sees you."

"I thought she liked me." She had spent many long afternoons with Yigal's mother, drinking tea, feeding the goldfish, making mayonnaise. Mrs Lipski insisted that mayonnaise had to be made by hand, drop by drop, and while Rebecca whisked the eggy mixture, Mrs Lipski would recite all the things she'd do as soon as Yigal got out of the army. "Afterwards," she'd begin with a jerk of the neck. Afterwards, she'd paint the house. Take a trip. Cut her hair.

"She likes you," Yigal said, nodding.

"Only you don't."

Yigal didn't answer, just continued lacing up his boots.

That's when Rebecca noticed the gun sticking out from under the bed. She leaned over and picked it up.

Yigal grabbed it from her. "It's not a toy." Then he stood up, slinging the gun over his shoulder.

"I thought you were staying overnight."

He stood in his baggy faded fatigues, looking down.

"Don't worry. You can have your bed. I'll leave."

He looked straight at her, for the first time since their lovemaking. "I must get back to my unit. I have a funeral tomorrow morning. And I must see the parents today. It is a custom with us."

Rebecca tried to say something, anything, but all she could do was reach for his leg. He pulled away and walked out, boots banging on the tiled floor.

She heard them on the broken walk outside, and then, for the longest time, on the road. Curled up in the patch of sun on her bed, she could almost make believe they were moving toward her and not away.

2.
INSIDE OUT

On the balcony off her bedroom, Rebecca drowsed in her sleeping bag. She listened to the scrape of furniture against tile, the clink of a metal pail. Every Thursday morning her land-lady, Mrs Bozo, had an Arab woman from the Old City in to wash her floors. Rebecca was supposed to keep an eye out to make sure that the old woman didn't steal anything. Not that Rebecca believed for one moment that Mrs Bozo thought her capable of instilling fear in even a toothless *aravia*. Rather, she supposed that her presence was intended to serve as a reminder to the old Arab that Mrs Bozo herself was never really out of sight. She was just ten yards away, in the adjoining apartment block, where her job was to clean Mrs Sheked's flat and take care of the young mother's toddler. Even now, through the ornate iron bars of her balcony railing, Rebecca could see Mrs Bozo mopping the floor of a living room that was the mirror-image of Mrs Bozo's own, right down to the scraggly philodendron tacked up the wall and across the ceiling. Rebecca thought: it's like listening to the television in one flat and watching the picture in another.

The doorbell rang. Rebecca crawled out of her sleeping bag and hurried inside. Most mornings Ethan came for her and together they would walk across the wadi to the university.

But by the time she reached the living room, Ethan was already tiptoeing toward her over the wet floor. He held his arms high over his head as if this was going to lessen the damage. The Arab woman, barefoot and beak-nosed, the hem of her embroidered black dress dripping water, erased his foot prints, one by one.

"You're not dressed," Ethan said, his arms still in the air.

Rebecca noticed the gaze of the woman shift from the floor to Rebecca's dress, as if she understood. Instead of a nightgown Rebecca slept in a long embroidered dress, almost identical to the one the old woman had on except that Rebecca's had faded from black to a purplish grey from repeated washing.

"You can put down your hands," Rebecca said, rubbing her aching eyes and turning back to her room. Ethan followed. Inside the room, he closed the door, got down on all fours and scuttled to his usual place in the corner where Mrs Bozo couldn't see him. Rebecca was not allowed to have men in her room.

"*Nu?*" Ethan drummed his fingers on the tile floor.

"I couldn't sleep, even out on the balcony." She opened her cupboard and stared at the almost-empty shelves. "There must have been a dog in heat. The street dogs were howling like crazy, thumping against the door. I was sure it would break. Or someone would run out with a broom. But nothing, not a peep from anyone. The sun was already coming up by the time I dozed off."

"So why didn't you go inside?" Ethan tipped Rebecca's trash bin toward him and grimaced. Bread crusts, discolored yoghurt containers, and bunched up green airgrams, never mailed.

"I told you I can't sleep in this bed. I think Mrs Bozo washes my sheets in disinfectant." With its bare walls, tile floor, narrow bed and white sheets, the room looked like a school infirmary. The day after she moved in, Mrs Bozo had stripped Rebecca's sheepskin rug off the floor, her embroidered spread off the bed, and placed them outside on the balcony where the sleeping bag had already been stored. One couldn't be too careful about body lice, Mrs Bozo insisted. Everyone knows why Arab men are always scratching themselves.

Ethan sighed. "I don't want to say it but. . ."

"Then don't," Rebecca said, turning her back on him.

"Admit it. You would never have taken the room if the name on the door was Schwartz or Goldstein. But Bozo. That's exactly why you wanted it. You knew it would be terrible."

"But not this terrible," she said, despising herself for the whine that had crept into her voice. Ethan was right. She had only herself to blame. She had taken Mrs Bozo's room because it was the opposite of everything she loved about the Lipskis. The overrun garden with the goldfish pool. The metal-hinged shutters that squeaked with the least wind. The servant's bedroom. She had promised herself that from now on she'd be as tough as the shine on Mrs Bozo's new tile floors.

"Re-be-caaaaa!"

Rebecca whirled around. Mrs Bozo, her pants hiked up to her knees, was wringing out a floor rag over the opposite balcony railing. "Everything okay?" she shouted across in Hebrew.

"Tell her her *aravia* just ran off with her Blaupunkt television," Ethan said.

Rebecca flashed Mrs Bozo an A-okay.

"And today make sure she washes your floor. Last week I had to wash it myself."

This time Rebecca smiled, an involuntary tug of her lips she couldn't explain, but was increasingly aware of.

As soon as Mrs Bozo turned away, Ethan snapped his fingers. "Get dressed already, will you? Mrs Bozo handles a rag the way Shiites handle testicles."

Though she and Ethan hadn't slept together since the Tuesday she returned to find Yigal asleep in her bed, she still felt comfortable about changing in front of him. But staring into her almost empty cupboard she could find nothing she wanted to change into.

"Let's do some business," Mrs Bozo had suggested that very first day Rebecca moved in. Mrs Bozo was sitting on Rebecca's bed, watching her unpack. "Four months free rent in return for your clothes."

Rebecca turned around. "My clothes?" Fat-cheeked and busty, but with thin, knobby legs, Mrs Bozo reminded her of a cabbage on a stick.

"Except these." With a quick, almost delicate flick of the wrist, Mrs Bozo plucked the embroidered Arab dress, some shorts and a mini-dress from the pile. "Not the style," she added, shaking her head.

Embarrassed, she didn't quite know why, Rebecca replied, "If there's something you really want, you can have it."

"Five months. But then I also get these," she said, fingering the flowery cotton sheets Rebecca imagined would always smell of Yigal.

For the first time Rebecca felt that strange smile — as if her habit of chewing her lips had metamorphosed into the habit of smiling. "Honestly. . . I don't think we wear the same size clothes."

"Let me worry about that." Already Mrs Bozo was scooping up the clothes, the sheets, her chin clamping down on the pile like a third arm.

Only later, when Rebecca saw her Lord & Taylor knit dress hanging from the downstairs clothesline, her magenta shirtwaist on the skinny wife of Pinchas the grocer, did she begin to understand. And even then she needed the arrival of Mrs Bozo's new Blaupunkt television, remote control, to grasp the extent of the woman's windfall.

"I'm not changing," Rebecca blurted out to Ethan. "I'm going like this." She slammed her cupboard door and headed for the bathroom.

When she returned, Ethan was reading a crumpled letter he'd retrieved from her trash bin. She grabbed it away.

"Hey — that was rather poetic," he said.

She looked at the soiled airgram. Like all the others in the bin, it was addressed to Michael. *What I'd really like is to walk out of here and go straight to the airport. End of my junior year abroad. Remember the first time I came for a weekend at Yale? You looked at my overnight case and asked if that meant you had to get me a motel room. The next weekend I came with panties and a toothbrush in my pocketbook. Well, I'd come to you now the same way, and not just because I want you so badly, though of course I do. The truth is everything I came with is gone. Stripped clean, sucked dry, turned inside out. That's me. To think that barely four months ago I was a person of weight. Someone to be reckoned with. At least I'm sure I never smiled. I mean SMILED, like some dolly bird...* She crumpled up the letter and tossed it back into the trash. "Let's go."

"You're not really serious about wearing that."

She looked down. The embroidered bodice was almost threadbare. There were gaps in the seams. "I'm not going to class. I'm going to meet Yigal," she mumbled.

"To get shtupped by a horny soldier, you didn't have to move. You were doing just fine where you were. At least you had a bed under your ass."

"You're pretty poetic yourself," she said, reaching for her string shopping bag. Now that she and Yigal

— 33 —

had begun to meet in the Jerusalem Forest, she liked to bring along some food. It made their meetings seem more like a picnic.

"Come on, Rivkele. Get hold of yourself. You're like a washed-up gambler who can't let go."

There was a silence. No doubt as a reminder of his dual heritage, Ethan had the annoying habit of tossing out gambler analogies whenever he wanted to sound lofty and profound.

Well?" he said, glowing with self-righteousness.

Rebecca listened to the padding of bare feet, the swish of a wet cloth. Suddenly, she pulled open the bedroom door. "In here, too," Rebecca said in Hebrew to the old woman.

The Arab looked up, expressionless. Her mop didn't stop for a second.

Rebecca flung her hand toward her bed. "Here! Here!" she repeated in English. But it was the same as last week. The woman ignored her.

"Shit on you, too!" Rebecca finally said and pushed past her, out the front door.

At the corner grocery she and Ethan parted. Ethan shook his head and sighed. Rebecca promised that she'd catch up with him later.

Except for Pinchas the owner, the grocery was empty. The morning rush was over and not even the housewives were thinking about lunch. A radio on a shelf blasted the nine o'clock news. Rebecca waited until the broadcast was over before she asked Pinchas for 100 grams of olives to go along with the rolls and cheese already in her string bag. The only etiquette she'd been able to ascertain in her four months here had to do with the news: whenever you heard it, in a grocery, a restaurant, on a bus, you kept your mouth shut until it was over.

Pinchas scooped the olives out of a plastic container, his eyes on her face. "What's the problem, sweetheart?" he finally said. "Too many late nights?"

Touching what she imagined were the huge raccoon-like circles around her eyes, she said, "Dogs. Did you hear them last night?"

"Dogs," he repeated, and set down the bag of olives.

She nodded. Again, she noticed Pinchas's eyes, deep set and green, with lashes so thick they made her feel as if she were looking in through a mesh screen. The sagging middle-aged jaw only made the eyes more remarkable.

"Ah!" His face rippled with understanding. "Dogs. The bitches pull them." Inexplicably to Rebecca, he said the last sentence in English.

"Pull?"

"You know, pull, pull." Slowly, he spread his

hands apart, then brought them together fast.

"Attract, you mean." Again she found herself smiling.

He shrugged. "Attract. Pull. Same thing. English just has more words."

"I didn't know you spoke any English," she said, reaching for the olives.

"My first wife was an American, from Baltimore." With pursed lips, he sucked in air. "I cried when she told me she was leaving. I was crazy for her. Go home if you want, I told her, but I'm never giving you a divorce." Falling back into Hebrew, he added, "I'm a traditional man. My uncle was a rabbi."

"But you did," Rebecca said looking around for the skinny woman who had bought her magenta dress from Mrs Bozo.

"Two years after Baltimore leaves, her father shows up at my door. He's holding a check for ten thousand dollars." Pinchas shrugged. "A man has to live. Besides, who's complaining? Now I have a grocery, a good wife, four children and one on the way." Pointing to the ceiling, he added, "Poor thing, she throws up everything. Even toast."

Rebecca opened her purse and paid. She could feel his eyes on her again, but this time on her dress. She wondered if he knew that his wife's new dress had once belonged to her.

"And, sweetheart," Pinchas said, dropping the money in the till, "any time you need anything, anything you forgot to buy on Shabbat, come upstairs. I'll open up the shop for you." Leaning closer, he added, "Only no cigarettes."

She looked up. Pinchas was so close now that she could see the gold flecks in the green. "Why not?"

"Surely you know it's forbidden to smoke on the Sabbath."

Rebecca caught sight of Yigal in the playground at the base of the forest. Rumpled, unshaven, he sat on a picnic table, a newspaper open on his lap, a cigarette slanting down his chin. Near his feet, propped against the bench, was a submachine gun. Obviously, he'd come straight from base. If it were the other way around, and he were on his way back to base, his uniform would be crisp and he'd have that little-kid washed-behind-the-ears look.

She crossed the sand pit where old women were stuffing curly-haired toddlers with bites of banana, and stopped. Yigal looked up, eyes narrowed from the smoke.

Rebecca smiled. "Hi."

"Hello." He stubbed out his cigarette, folded his newspaper, and stood up. She wondered if he was going to kiss her, but he lifted up his knapsack and newspaper in one hand, the gun in the other.

"You've been waiting long?" she asked as they headed away from the playground, toward the pine hillside.

He shrugged. "Not too bad. I had a good lift in this morning." He spoke English with a combination British-German accent, which somehow suited his formal attitude. Each time they met, it was as if they were strangers all over again. "I even had time to eat breakfast," he added.

"Oh, I thought we could eat together. I brought us some cheese and rolls. And olives." She held up her string bag.

"You may eat if you like." They started walking up the log steps carved into the hillside. The only concession he made to her presence was that every few steps, he'd stop and wait for her to catch up.

"I'm not really hungry," she said, toeing a cluster of shiny mushrooms. Last week Yigal had promised to explain the different varieties to her, show her how to tell which ones she could pick and eat, but he hadn't had time. He'd had to be back at his base in the north by noon.

"How was your week?" she asked. "I heard about that raid from Metulla over the border into Syria. And thought of you," she added tentatively. She'd never tell him that as soon as she'd heard the midnight BBC broadcast, which reported two dead, four wounded, no names pending notification of families, she had walked across Jerusalem to his house. The buses had stopped running and she didn't have enough cash for a taxi. She knew that if his lights were on, if cars were out front, something had happened. If it was dark, he was all right. The whole way she kept saying, "Please let it be dark. Please God, let it be dark." It was dark. By the time she got back to Mrs Bozo's, the bread trucks were already making their morning rounds.

"The raid was into Lebanon. How can you go from Metulla into Syria? Haven't you ever bothered to look at a map?"

Rebecca felt her smile swell, forcing her lips up at the corners, pressing against her cheeks. Suddenly she knew why she smiled so much over here. She was unhappy, nervous about being unhappy. Israelis had their cigarettes, Americans had their smiles.

"You *amerika'im* take nothing seriously. Everything's a joke."

She tossed her head. "Yes. Even my dress. Like it?" Before he could answer, she added, "Actually, it's my nightgown."

He stared, his eyes narrowing to green slits.

She lifted up her dress and twirled around. She

had no underwear on.

Laughing, he reached out and caught her by the hips. His newspaper fell to the ground. "Crazy *amerika'it*."

"Leave me alone!" She pushed him so hard, two hands against his chest, that he stumbled backward. After a moment's silence, he bent over and picked up his newspaper, set it under his arm, and turned to leave. But even before he took a step, she caught him by the arm.

It was late afternoon by the time Rebecca arrived back at Mrs Bozo's. Today, she hadn't even bothered to ask Yigal to explain the different types of mushrooms to her. Picking dead pine needles and grit from his knees, he told her that his mother was expecting him for lunch, was leaving work early to be with him. After he left, she stayed behind. She had semen stains on the back of her dress, and even after they dried she still couldn't bear the thought of taking a bus, being with people. Even Ethan.

At five o'clock the courtyard outside Mrs Bozo's apartment block was filled with people, laughing, gossiping, eating. Mouths never closed, hands never still. Rebecca spotted her knit dress and linen slacks seated together on a bench, and only afterward Mrs

Bozo beside them, head wagging, hands zipping through the air. Rebecca hurried across the courtyard, head lowered, arms across her chest. A path opened in front of her.

In her room she dropped onto her bed. But even as she pressed her face into the pillow, she heard a high-pitched yelping. She recognized the sound of a dog in pain. Pushing herself up off the bed, she staggered to her open balcony door. On the slope between the adjoining apartment blocks, she saw two dogs stuck together at the genitals. The female, not much more than a puppy, was being dragged from behind by the male, a splotched street dog with a pink snout. The puppy's hind feet didn't even reach the ground. Her face scraped the dirt. A few people looked on, smirking, shaking their heads, pulling away their children. But nobody did anything.

Rebecca hurried to the kitchen and grabbed a metal tray of ice cubes from the freezer. She dumped them into Mrs Bozo's fancy dish towel that was just for show. She remembered hearing that ice cubes applied to the testicles would do the trick.

Even in the stairwell, she could hear the puppy's yelps. She hiked up her dress and took the steps two at a time.

On the slope now, she could see the dull, remote face of the male. He'd finished his business, wanted to get on, but it was the female who'd wrapped herself around him, her fear that held him tight. Crouching down, Rebecca took aim with her ice pack. But as she reached underneath, the puppy snapped, her teeth sinking into the flesh of her thumb.

"Crazy bitch!" Rebecca dropped the ice pack and kicked the puppy in the ribs. She was about to kick her again when she felt a restraining hand on her shoulder.

"She's nervous, she's too young, she should never have been let out alone," Rebecca heard a woman say. Turning around, she was face to face with Mrs Bozo.

"But I wanted to help." Rebecca looked at her hand. There were tooth marks and blood.

Mrs Bozo pulled a tissue out of her dress sleeve and pressed it to the bite. "You were very brave."

Rebecca felt the warm rush of tears. She didn't fight them. Instead, she looked through them at the strange group that had gathered around and was pressing in on her. The woman in Rebecca's linen pants was dabbing the bite with ice cubes from the dish towel. The woman in the knit was shaking a bottle of iodine. A man she'd never seen before was wiping her cheeks with his handkerchief. Mr Sheked was saying he'd drive her to the clinic. To

Rebecca, each offer, each gift, was wonderful, and suddenly her belongings, scattered now among all her neighbors, seemed to be no longer valuables she'd been cheated out of, but gifts she, too, had freely given.

Mrs Bozo and Mr Sheked led Rebecca to the car, each holding her firmly by the arm, as if she might suddenly change her mind and run.

3.
PILGRIMS

With a pink marker Rebecca highlighted each unfamiliar word she came across in that morning's *Yediot Aharonot*. The one time she managed an entire paragraph without resort to her pink pen she found herself musing about switching to the tonier *Ha'aretz*, which was the newspaper the little grey-suited man across from her was reading — when he wasn't peering at her over the top of the page. He had small, intense eyes, the same blue-grey as his woolen jacket. A retired schoolteacher, she decided, who had come here to escape an empty unheated flat. She'd noticed that on winter days like today the university library was full of old men. With their woolen jackets and fedoras, their newspapers and tobacco smells, they gave the place the atmosphere of a high-class coffee shop.

She was aware of the old man smiling as she

began to transcribe the new words in her childish Hebrew hand. She bore down harder. She'd learned that in this country eye contact was dangerous. Israelis took it as an invitation to tell you the sorts of things that strangers back home kept to themselves. Like you had an ink smudge on your cheek. Or your hem was coming down.

She was so absorbed in fending off the old man's stubborn smile that she didn't hear the whistling. Not until his knuckles came down on the table and he scolded in a precise, schoolmasterly voice: "You should be ashamed of yourself, young man."

Rebecca looked up. Ethan was swinging in from the aisle, whistling under his breath. He looked scruffy and worn, his hair in need of a good washing. Even the ridiculous red bandanna around his neck looked soiled.

"Sorry, I don't speak Hebrew," Ethan answered the old man, beaming as if he'd been complimented. With the same idiotic expression, he turned to Rebecca: "Jeez, I've been looking all over for you."

"Jeez, well here I am," she answered coldly. And it wasn't just this spectacle she held against him. For two weeks now she'd been spending her days in the library with her newspapers and dictionaries and assorted old men.

— 46 —

"This is a place of study," the man interrupted in German-accented English. For emphasis, he reached across the table and jabbed Rebecca's newspaper.

Ethan regarded the pink-streaked newsprint. "Well, well. And I figured you'd found yourself another soldier."

The old man's thin chest puffed up. But before he could come to Rebecca's rescue, she threw her things together, got up, and headed for the door.

Ethan followed, still whistling.

Outside the reading room, she turned on him. "So what do you want?"

He looked hurt. "Since when do I have to want something to talk to you?"

"I'm sorry," she said, softening. How many times those first months had she called him up, rung his doorbell, dragged him out of bed, all because she'd needed someone to talk to? "I just wish you didn't have to exaggerate." She gave a tug on his bandanna. God knows where he'd picked it up. She knew his clothes as well as she knew her own.

"*Me* exaggerate? What about this?" He returned her tug, but on her pony tail. Lately she'd taken to wearing her hair up, off her neck, soldier-girl style. "Not to mention this." He picked up her hundred-pound dictionary and gave her a whack on the behind.

She walked away.

"I don't blame you though," Ethan said, catching up with her at the front door. "It's this country that's to blame. It exaggerates. Makes us exaggerate."

Outside the library, he tipped his chin at the building's huge windowless facade. "I mean just look at that. A fucking fifty-foot menorah. In America Chanukah meant something."

Rebecca glanced up and shrugged. At this angle the scatter of light bulbs seemed almost random.

"I don't even know why I bother. What the hell do you know about Chanukah in America?"

She chose not to answer. The first time she told Ethan she used to hang up a Christmas stocking, he thought she was joking. Just as she thought it was a joke when he told her that his father was a rabbi in Las Vegas.

"You think it's all just dandy, don't you?"

She regarded him. It suddenly struck her that somehow these past weeks their roles had reversed. Before she was the one comparing, complaining, refusing to accept. Now it was Ethan. "Hey, take it easy," she said, reaching for his arm. "It's only a bunch of light bulbs."

"Exactly," he muttered.

They fell into step across the almost deserted

courtyard. The mist was so thick she couldn't make out the black iron gates or the guards at the entrance. She didn't even think about where they were going. It was suddenly enough that they were together, wasting time.

"It would be nice if it snows," Ethan said and started whistling. She suddenly recognized the tune he had been whistling in the library: "White Christmas."

"One of your subtle hints?"

"I thought you forgot."

"I did." December 24. She must have seen it on the newspaper, but if she had, it hadn't registered.

"Well, I didn't. I was even going to surprise you with tickets to Bethlehem, but *they* wouldn't let me have any."

"Why not?"

"They're reserved for pilgrims. Not Jews. Not Hippies." He pronounced it "eepies," the way an Israeli would.

She laughed. "Don't tell me you've got no *protect-zia* in the tourist ministry? Not one lousy cousin?" Wherever they went, it seemed, Ethan (or Eitan as his family called him) was besieged by some cousin or cousin-of-a-cousin eager to ask a favor or bestow one.

He slowed and halted. "I'm afraid you're the only

protectzia I've got," he said, touching her chin.

She was about to bring up Bjorn, a freeloading Swede with whom Ethan spent all of his time these past weeks and who was the reason for her retreat to the library. But she couldn't bear to appear jealous or needy.

"You're such a nice girl, Miss Harrison, with such a nice nice name." Ethan tucked a loose blond lock behind her ear. "A pilgrim." From his pocket, he fished out a short string of smooth amber beads.

"Worry beads?"

"Your rosary, my dear."

She started laughing. "They'll never buy it," she said, reaching for the beads anyway.

"You kidding? Those fools will never know the difference."

The day was so dark that Rebecca kept thinking it was later than it was. Finally, she suggested they go early to Bethlehem and splurge on dinner. She hadn't eaten a real meal since Bjorn turned up at Ethan's apartment, a turnip-shaped man with a donkey bag tied around his middle, bragging that he'd smoked hashish with King Hussein's nephew.

At the Old City bus station she and Ethan huddled together, blowing out and watching their breath mingle like children who aren't used to the cold. The mist had turned to drizzle, and the evening air had a wet, doggy odor. Their hands, linked in Ethan's pocket, were warm and sticky. Though they hadn't slept together since the summer, they still sometimes held hands.

The bus to Bethlehem wasn't a modern Egged bus with soda advertisements, but a real banger from English Mandate days. The tourists would arrive later in specially chartered heated buses. These passengers were almost all Arab workmen, heads wrapped, plastic carriers of food and workclothes at their side. The bus filled with the smell of cement.

Rebecca scanned the floor and overhead rack for suspicious packages, but every carrier looked like every other, so she gave up and looked out the window. The road to Bethlehem was only four or five miles, but it always felt much longer. With a knot in her stomach, she stared at the apartment blocks of reinforced concrete, no windows facing south, just bathroom vents, waiting for the bump on the road that marked the old border. The two sections of highway were uneven, and not even the new strip of tar could make them meet. After the bump everything suddenly stopped: no blocks of flats or parking lots or tricycles. No mothers on benches, rocking carriages and stuffing children with bananas. Only the terraced hills, silvery rings of olive trees and stone.

Rebecca pressed her forehead against the window. At the base of a ravine, she could make out a stone house with a walled orchard, an Arab on a mule, twigs strapped to the animal's side.

She squeezed their linked hands, still in Ethan's pocket. "Doesn't it look like something straight out of the Bible?" she murmured.

He looked past her out the window. "Since when do they have housing projects in the *Tanach*?"

She peered again. In the distance she could make out stone towers rising up like children's blocks out of a gouged-out hill. Gilo. A couple of months before there had been only orange-roped squares and a parking lot of cut stone.

They left the Bethlehem bus station with its soldiers and policemen and hawkers, and settled on a little restaurant with green formica tables and a refrigerated food display. A kerosene heater smoked beside the cashier. Arab music drifted in from the kitchen. They ordered hummus and shashlik and french fries and nonalcoholic black beer. Rebecca swore she'd never been so hungry. Eating fast, much faster than Ethan, she began to tell him about an Arab girl in her summer Hebrew class, who on the last day had invited everyone to her house in

Bethlehem.

"It was above the family dry goods store. We sat in these big yellow velvet chairs. There must have been eight of them, all identical, in one room. Her mother served us Turkish coffee in gold-rimmed cups from Germany. But none of us knew what to say. So we just sat there smiling until it was time to go."

From the way Ethan's eyes wandered, to a party of Germans, to the cashier, to a journalist jotting notes, she knew he wasn't listening. She finally shut up. In the plate-glass store front she studied their reflection: the back of Ethan's head, and her own sharp-featured face a bit to the side and above it. Then some soldiers stopped in front of the window and the image melted into their green jackets.

"What's wrong?" Ethan said at last.

Rebecca regarded him. "Maybe you'll tell me."

"Maybe," Ethan said, quirking his eyebrows. But he didn't go on and they lapsed into another silence. Damned if she was going to say anything. After all, it wasn't as if *she* had dragged *him*.

After maybe five minutes, Ethan said, "You know what your problem is?"

She looked up. "No, please tell me."

"You want to be the center of attention all the

time. Let someone even look someplace else and you take it as a personal insult. I've noticed that about you."

She flushed. Whatever transformation had taken hold of him, one thing sure as hell hadn't changed: the urge to pontificate. "If you really want to get into problems," she said, clenching her teeth. "All you're interested in is in acting like a jerk. The only reason you wanted to come is because some fucking Israeli bureaucrat didn't want you to." She pulled the beads from her pocket and rattled them. "You don't give a damn about being here." She paused. "With me or anyone else."

"How would you know *what* I give a damn about? I could've come in barking today and you wouldn't have noticed." He tried to grab the beads, but she snatched them away.

"Uh, uh, mine," she said, pocketing them.

For some moments they just glared at each other. Then at the same time they started laughing.

The German tourists turned to stare. Rebecca caught the word, "hippy".

"I really hate that bandanna," Rebecca said, returning to her food.

"Bjorn gave it to me before he left."

She looked up, her fork paused in mid-air. "You didn't tell me he left."

He smiled. "You never asked."

Manger Square was lit up like a baseball stadium. Television crews aimed their cameras from specially constructed wooden platforms. Soldiers with guns and walkie-talkies looked down from the rooftops. Arab kids with olive-wood souvenirs stuffed under their jackets pushed through the crowd, ducking under barricades and past guards. "What you want, lady? I got cheap."

The cold air turned stale. Rebecca could smell the vinyl rain hat of the woman in front of her, could hear the French woman behind her clearer than she could hear Ethan. Then the singing began. Despite everything—the lights, the hustlers, the soldiers—she found herself strangely moved, wanting to join in, but not letting herself. Ethan did. She had never heard him sing before, and she was surprised at how powerful his voice was. Even more that he seemed to know all the words. She leaned into his shoulder and closed her eyes.

The service over, they followed a group of pilgrims onto their bus and scrunched down in the velour seats at the rear, warming their toes on the heating vents. When the bus stopped in front of a church hostel in the Old City, they took off before the driver knew what was up.

Rebecca was lost, but Ethan didn't hesitate. He led her up and down alleys she was surprised he could follow, especially at night.

"Where are we going?" she asked.

"You'll see."

Rebecca was exhausted, but she allowed Ethan to pull her along. He seemed so sure of himself tonight, so in control, almost like those first months when he'd played spiritual as well as physical guide. After leading her through a cramped courtyard, he steered her down an open stone staircase decorated in fluorescent paint. As soon as he opened the door, the smell of mold hit her. In the cave-like interior, she stumbled over a pillow and knocked into a low brass tray. Some greasy men looked up and laughed. "Talk about scum," she said as they finally flopped down in an alcove illumined by a candle in a Coke bottle. "How did you find this place?"

"Actually Bjorn found it." Ethan dipped his finger into the puddle of wax at the top of the candle and watched it turn hard.

"Great recommendation." The men were still laughing. As far as she could tell, she was the only woman.

"Not your type, huh?"

"Parasites are not my cup of tea." She hesitated. "Besides, he couldn't stand me." Whenever she would come for Ethan, Bjorn would keep her waiting in the hall. Until finally she stopped coming.

"Maybe you weren't his cup of tea either."

Rebecca became aware of someone looking at them and glanced up. A slim mustached man in a shiny white jersey was slouched against a pillar. Even the waiters look foxy, she thought. "Come on, let's order so we can get out of here."

"What's your rush? When I don't talk, you think I'm ignoring you. And when I do, you don't want to listen." Ethan peeled the wax off his finger and rolled it into a ball. "Besides, the action only begins about now. Would you believe that last night I actually saw a Hasid here?"

"You were here last night?"

There was a pause.

"He sat right over there." Ethan flicked the wax off his finger. It landed with a ping on the neighboring table.

"But it's not even kosher," she said, shaking her head.

"You know what they tell the boys in the yeshiva? If you got to do it, do it out of your neighborhood. Don't bring shame on your family, your school."

"I think there'd be better places to find a woman,"

she said, shooting a quick glance around the place again.

Ethan smiled, just the slightest. "He was looking for a man."

A moment passed. Rebecca heard another burst of male laughter. Leave it to Bjorn to find a joint like this.

"He was in there maybe fifteen minutes," Ethan continued, gesturing to the opposite alcove, which contained a plywood door. "He came out with his face all red, his black coat bunched up in back. A few seconds later a little Arab followed him out."

"Poor bastard." Rebecca sank back against the pillowed wall and closed her eyes. She listened to Ethan drumming his fingers on the metal tray.

"There he is now."

She thought Ethan meant the Hasid, but when she opened her eyes, she saw the foxy man in the shiny jersey she had mistaken for a waiter. He was looking at Ethan.

"Let's get out of here." Rebecca stood up quickly, knocking against the tray and toppling the candle.

Ethan picked up the candle. She watched the flame sputter.

"There was no Hasid, was there?" she murmured. "It was you."

Ethan stared at her and replaced the candle in the

bottle holder.

The taxi dropped them at the apartment Ethan shared with four other American students. As they got out, the driver wished them "Happy Christmas" and winked.

"If you want to, I will," Rebecca said as she closed the bedroom door behind them.

"You really don't understand." He flopped down on the unmade bed. Exhausted, she kicked off her shoes and stretched out beside him. He reached an arm around her.

"It's not you," she said, nestling into him. "It's this country. It exaggerates. It makes us exaggerate. Just like you said. Me and Yigal. You and Bjorn. Don't you see? It's all connected."

He started stroking her cheek. "We're connected," he said after a minute or two.

She covered his hand with her own. "Because we're in this together."

"This?" He sounded amused, or maybe just confused.

"This year. . . seeing where it takes us. . . ." She yawned, too tired to go on. Her legs were drifting off. She wanted to follow.

She knew he said something more because she could feel the vibration in his chest, but the words never reached her.

Rebecca awoke alone. She listened for the rooster she remembered from the summer. On those Sabbaths she'd spent with Ethan, she used to love waking up to the animal sounds that drifted up from the wadi. She knew there was a North African development beneath them, she'd seen the asbestos huts from the bus, but from Ethan's window all she could see was the mounded dirt of a bulldozed hill.

Ethan was waiting for her in the dining corner, showered and changed, hair slicked back, no bandanna. The table was set for two, with fresh rolls and a brass coffee service. She had the identical service in her room, gathering dust. They had bought them in the Old City, "two for the price of one," the day they had become lovers.

"I didn't hear the rooster," she said, feeling shy in a way she never had with him before.

"Probably ended up in someone's soup." Ethan held out a tiny cup of coffee in a tarnished brass holder.

"Thanks." She took the coffee and sat down. For the first time she noticed someone in a sleeping bag sacked out on the living room floor. "Bjorn sell his place?" she was tempted to say. But everything about this morning, Ethan all spiffed up, the fresh rolls and cardamon-scented coffee, her own shyness, hinted at a fragility so beautiful, so pure, she wanted nothing to endanger it. "You got up early," she said, smiling.

"I couldn't sleep. I thought I'd surprise you," he added, refilling his cup to match hers.

Wordlessly, they clinked cups and drank.

"So what's the celebration?" she said, grimacing in spite of herself. The coffee tasted tinny. Probably the finjon was meant just for show.

"A going away party."

He said it quietly, his lips barely moving, but she heard it like a line in a movie, loud, pointed, with an exaggerated pause before and after.

"You can't."

"What's to stop me?"

"Me?" She tried to smile.

He touched her cheek. "So come with me. I thought about it all last night. It can work."

A moment passed. Then another. "Where?"

"Paris. I made my reservation yesterday. Before the Christmas tickets," he added, as if the distinction was important.

"Paris," she repeated. She suddenly wondered if maybe this was her real destination, if what she'd assumed all these months was a road would turn out to be just a detour.

"And then on to Monte Carlo. Why not give them a run for their money? Show them what a rabbi's son from Las Vegas can do?"

She smiled in spite of herself. But a moment later the sleeping bag began to wriggle and stretch like a green cocoon, and all the ugly feelings of yesterday and the day before returned. She had an urge to get up and stomp on it. Why of all the floors in the world did Bjorn have to choose this one to crash?

"I can't breathe in here," she said, getting up. She felt a squeezing in her chest, as if her heart were being wrung out like one of Mrs Bozo's floor rags. "I can't think."

Outside, she breathed deep. It was a winter day without a hint of yesterday's bitter mist. Blue skies, hot sun. The first red anemones sprouted from crevices, sidewalk edges, wherever they could gain a hold.

"Well, Rivkele?" Ethan said.

"I've never been down there," she murmured, looking past him to the wadi below. She suddenly grabbed his hand and pulled. "Come on." And when he didn't budge, she added, "Hey, I went with you yesterday. Now you come with me."

Laughing, they made their way down the bull-dozed ravine, sliding, tripping, balancing each other. When they approached the animal pen at the base, an old woman with dark skin and white hair stopped beating her mattress and hurried inside. She watched them from an open window until they began their descent into the second, even deeper, wadi.

The terraced slopes, untouched by bulldozers, reminded Rebecca of stone bleachers in a huge am-phitheater. She couldn't see the bottom. She leaped from terrace to terrace. "I can't believe I've never come here before," she kept saying, over and over. She knew the old border had to be close, but she had no idea where. When she spotted the flash of ribbon across the wadi bed, she thought of a stream, even though she knew there could be no such thing in the Judaean Hills. Only after a couple minutes did she recognize railroad tracks. She had never taken the railroad here. Nowadays nobody did, except soldiers, who traveled free and didn't care how long it took to get back to base.

"Let's follow the tracks," she shouted, dropping Ethan's hand and racing on ahead. She remembered hearing that before '48 the railroad had linked Beirut and Cairo.

By the time she reached the tracks, Ethan still

hadn't caught up. She tied her sweater around her waist and walked on alone. Before long, coming toward her, she saw two Arab workmen, heads wrapped in kafiahs, carriers at their side. She considered waiting up for Ethan, but instead she found herself walking even faster, arms swinging at her side.

As she passed the workmen, she nodded.

They just stared.

When she glanced back a moment later, they were still staring.

A few minutes later Ethan was beside her, red-faced and panting. "So what do you say, Rivkele? Paris? Monte Carlo?"

Rebecca looked up at the terraced hills rising up on either side of them. With a burst of energy, she broke into a run. But this time Ethan ran alongside, keeping pace on the railway ties. In his deep voice, he began to sing "I've been working on the railroad. . . " She joined in. Each time they finished they began again, each round louder than the one before.

She heard a whistle behind them, and glanced over at Ethan. He kept on the track, singing, not breaking pace. The whistle sounded again, sharp and loud this time, and then a rumbling. Her mouth was dry. She had a stitch in her ribs.

At the same moment they leaped, but to different sides, and in that final second before the train shrieked between them, they stared, wide-eyed and seemingly calm, like birds into an oncoming windshield.

4.
NEFESH HaGOLAN

Each time the overloaded tender hit a bump, the bottom scraped the road and everyone on the cargo floor said, "Whoa!"

"I wasn't expecting so many volunteers," the driver finally shouted back in Hebrew. "But it's good. Very good. Shimon will be happy."

On the dirt road into the settlement, the truck bogged down in the mud and stalled. Everyone got out into the cold evening drizzle and pushed. When they climbed back in, the cargo space filled with the smell of wet wool. To Rebecca it all seemed kind of cozy, the cramped darkness, the rain on the roof, even the doggy smell.

At seven o'clock someone up front switched on the radio. In response to the news beeps, the guy next to Rebecca shouted for the driver to turn up the volume. Even in Hebrew, she could detect his

South African accent. She had first noticed him on the bus ride from Jerusalem to Tiberias, a good-looking guy in a Fair Isle sweater, chatting up the girls. For the last hour they'd been sitting, bouncing, yawning shoulder-to-shoulder.

"Yeah Derek, tell us if we should make out our wills."

Rebecca recognized Sandy's voice. She and Sandy had been roommates for the first month. Sandy had arrived a plump virgin with pimples and a trunk full of toilet paper. By the end of August she had lost her virginity to a Moroccan she met on a bus. The baby fat she'd starved off. The toilet paper she'd sold off. Only her Bronx accent, it seemed, she couldn't get rid of.

The news over, Yardena, the group leader from the university, turned around in her seat. Rebecca couldn't make out her features, only the blunt line of her jaw against the fogged-up windshield.

"Before we arrive, I want to remind you that we are coming here to work, not play," she said in English. "Nefesh HaGolan means soul of the Golan. It is a new settlement, not even one year old. They have only eighteen members and are still in temporary houses. That means we have much to do these next days. So I hope no one here is expecting a vacation." With that, she settled back in her seat.

"*Arbeit macht frei*," the South African whispered into Rebecca's hair.

Not understanding, she assumed he'd said something in Afrikaans. She'd seen South Africans do that, start talking to each other in broken Afrikaans so that no one would understand. "I'm not South African," she said, her voice sticky after so many hours of silence.

She could feel him laughing. "It's German. 'Work makes you free'. You know, Auschwitz? The sign on the gate? She's got the voice for it. Looks, too."

A moment passed. She wasn't sure she liked him. "How long you been here?" she said at last.

"Three years." He lit up a cigarette. Rebecca caught a glimpse of blond mustache. "And you're like the other Americans? At the university on a one-year sentence?"

Sandy gave her no chance to reply. "Hey Derek," she cut in. "You don't really expect to hit on all eight of us with the same line, do you?"

"Be patient, Sandy," Derek sighed. "You'll get your turn."

At that moment the tender lurched to a stop. The driver climbed out and opened the rear loading door. They looked out across an expanse of mud to a flat-roofed prefab building. Ten or eleven men in hooded army jackets and black boots huddled under a lighted overhang. A few smoked. The others had their hands stuffed in their pockets.

"Forget it, Derek," Sandy said. "I'm not waiting around."

Ami, a short balding fellow with a limp, led them to their sleeping quarters, the old Syrian barracks from before '67. Sheets of heavy plastic covered the windows. Inside, scrawled on the walls in red paint, was Arabic writing. Here and there chunks of words were missing, the plaster blasted away.

Ami stooped to light the portable kerosene heater. Rebecca noticed that the sole of his right boot was a good four inches thick. "It's not exactly the Hilton," he mumbled, rolling the burnt match stick between his fingers. "But we also stayed here the first months."

Everyone wandered off between the neat rows of iron beds. Derek paused in the doorway of a small room off the main barracks. It had two beds and its own sink, and looked as if it might have been the officers' quarters. "Anyone interested in the bridal suite?" he asked. Turning, his eyes met Sandy's. "Sweetheart, with a little American ingenuity you could set up shop."

Sandy struck a pose, one hand on her head, the other on her hip. "I'm afraid it still wouldn't help you, Derek."

Hoots and whistles. Even before the ruckus died down, Stuart, the only other male in the group, paused in front of a porcelain sink. Its rounded lip was sheared away so that it stuck out like a shelf. "Hey, how's this for a urinal?" he said, crouching.

Yardena broke up the laughter with a stiff clapping of hands. "I suggest you each find a bed immediately so we may go to the dining hall," she said. "I'm going to sleep in the little room. Anyone else is welcome."

Derek wriggled his eyebrows at Stuart, who clutched his throat.

From the doorway, a few seconds later, Rebecca said to Yardena, "Mind if I join you?"

Yardena looked up. Rebecca noticed a tuck in her eyelid, an old scar, it looked like.

"As you wish."

In the dining hall the eighteen members of Nefesh HaGolan sat together along two narrow tables placed end to end. The only woman was a very pregnant redhead who tossed her head when she laughed. And she laughed a lot, Rebecca noticed, mostly with the man next to her, her husband, she supposed. At one point the man put two fingers to the woman's lips. "Shhhhhh".

But she went on laughing. "I don't know what I'm going to do with you," she said, shaking her head.

Something about the woman made Rebecca take a closer look at the man. He was tall and thin, with wet slicked-back hair and slightly rounded shoulders. Instead of work clothes, he had on a sky-blue turtleneck, fold marks still in the cloth. As Rebecca watched, the woman leaned over and bit off the white tag still threaded to the blue collar.

Rebecca found herself smiling for the first time since she had left Jerusalem.

After dinner, a ruddy, heavy-set man with woolly hair and crinkly eyes, stood up. Like everyone else at the table, he had a cigarette in his hand.

"Hello. My name is Shimon," he announced in English. "I'm head of Nefesh HaGolan. I want to welcome you. You're our first group of volunteers. If I told you how many papers I had to fill out to get you here. . . " He drew on his cigarette. "Well, good thing I've got something going with the secretary," he added, gesturing to the perky redhead.

She tossed her head.

Everyone laughed, even Rebecca. She told herself she should have guessed the woman wasn't married to the man in blue.

"Seriously, you've come at a very special time for

Nefesh HaGolan," Shimon continued. "Rahel is expecting any day now. The first baby in a settlement is very special, and belongs to all of us, and I hope, as our guests, a little to you, too. Welcome." He stuck the cigarette back in his mouth and sat down. The volunteers clapped.

"So I guess we know the previous occupants of your bridal suite," Derek said to Rebecca.

He was wedged between her and Sandy on the wooden bench. Even though she didn't particularly like him, she liked the feeling of his shoulder against her own, as if their cramped ride up the Golan Heights had left an imprint.

"Or at least one occupant," he added, smirking.

"What do you mean?" She watched Derek take out a cigarette and pack it against the back of his freckled hand.

"I mean she's quite the queen bee, isn't she?"

Rebecca stole a sideways peek at the woman. She was still laughing with the man in blue.

"What's this about queens, Derek?" Sandy helped herself to a cigarette. "You got a problem?"

Derek lit Sandy's cigarette with his own. "You know, honey, you're lucky you're pretty."

"No." She lifted her chin so that her cigarette drooped. "You're lucky I'm pretty."

Rebecca stood up, carried her dish and silverware

over to the plastic tub of soapy water, dropped them
in and walked out.

Hugging her shoulders, she wandered over to the
animal sheds a few hundred yards from the main
building. The air was cold and damp and thick with
the smell of manure. Her sneakers made a sucking
noise in the soft earth. At the sheep lean-to, she
stopped and peered inside. She couldn't see much,
just the flicker of animal eyes, but she could hear
nestling sounds, snug little grunts. With a pang she
thought of Ethan. The only communication she'd
had was a postcard from the Cote d'Azur, no words,
just a stick figure dripping a line of tears. The same
day she'd signed up to come here for winter break.
A mistake, she knew now. She would have been better off spending her vacation in the library as she
had originally planned.

On the way back to the barracks, she spotted a
yellow bulldozer and climbed up. The cab still gave
off a new-car smell. She settled back in the seat,
softer than she had expected, and closed her eyes. If
only she weren't so cold . . . she'd spend the night.

Before long, music began to drift over from one
of the prefabs. A radio, she assumed, until she
realized the same five or six songs were playing
over and over, always in the same order. Most of

them were old Beatles records. She hummed along. A party, she decided, someone was having a party. Not thirty feet away from her, people were leaning into each other, whispering, warm.

Footsteps suddenly rocked the cab and a light blinded her.

"What you doing here?"

An old, rattly voice spoke Hebrew, but Hebrew worse even than her own. She had been addressed as a man.

"I'm a volunteer." she said, raising her arm against the glare. All she could see were gold teeth. "Please, the light," she added.

The beam moved from her face to the fancy new dashboard. In the reflected glow she saw a wrinkled, gappy-mouthed Arab in a white kafiah and army greens. A submachine gun dangled from his shoulder. She gathered he must be a Druze guard.

"Not good outside," the man added, flashing the light in a wide arc. "Very bad weather."

Rebecca peered at the mist, so thick it looked like snow. She shivered. "The skies will clear tomorrow," she said, repeating a phrase she had just learned.

He shrugged.

She wondered if this meant he wasn't sure about the weather or didn't understand her Hebrew. Or didn't care.

She pointed to the sky. "Nice day tomorrow."

"Maybe." After a pause, the old man added, "Very very cold. You should go." Then the light went out, the cab rocked, and he was gone. She watched him head down toward the animal sheds. With only his kafiah visible he looked as if he were floating.

Then she climbed down, too.

The windows in the prefab building were high and square, and Rebecca had to stand on tiptoe to see in. Her first reaction was that she had made a mistake. The music couldn't be coming from this room. The only one in it was the man in the blue jersey. He was stretched out on the bed, legs crossed, smoking. Then she noticed a record player on the table beside him, and next to it a full crate of orange soda.

She rapped hard on the window, and ran as fast as she could.

The following morning was cold but clear. Ice crystals gathered in the folds of the plastic window covering. Slashes of sunlight fell across the cement floor.

"Your chore this morning is to clean the kitchen," Yardena said to Rebecca when she returned from the bathroom. The group leader was crouched down next to the kerosene heater, warming her hands over the pilot.

"The kitchen?" Rebecca watched the inky smoke curl up between Yardena's long fingers. "I'd really prefer to do something outside. Anything."

"We chose our chores last night after dinner. You left the group." Yardena looked up, eyes watery from the smoke.

Again Rebecca noticed the tuck in her eyelid.

"How should I know what you want to do?" Yardena added. "I'm not a mind reader."

Rebecca flushed and started for the door.

"Maybe you think it's none of my business," Yardena called after her. "But an *amerika'it* should really be more careful. This place is like an army camp."

Rebecca turned around. So that was it. Yardena assumed she had found her way into some guy's bed. "Thanks, I'll try to remember that," she answered, refusing to set her straight.

For part of the morning Rebecca shared the kitchen with two female soldiers. She didn't understand where they were from, or exactly why they'd come. She had gone out to the storeroom for a new bottle of ammonia, and when she returned, they were sitting on stools, pounding turkey cutlets and chattering away. Rebecca wondered if maybe they were traveling cooks, like temps in an office, but they didn't seem to know what they were doing. To each other, they kept saying things like, "How's this?" Occasionally, they glanced over at Rebecca and nodded. But they never addressed her.

Then, around eleven o'clock, a lanky soldier leaned into the kitchen and shouted, "Let's get moving!"

The girls motioned to Rebecca to watch the frying cutlets, picked up their pocketbooks and headed for the door. "Ciao!"

A few minutes later the man with the limp who had first shown them to the barracks shuffled in. "I hope she's a better driver than she is cook," Ami said, turning up the flame under the oil-soaked cutlets. "Or my brother can say goodbye to this world."

"There were two," said Rebecca.

He sighed. "With my brother there always are."

"Your brother's the soldier?"

"He came by to see where we're going to build the permanent houses. He's nice, no?" Patting his right leg, he added, "He got all the inches I lost."

"Did it happen in the war?"

"Polio," he said, flipping a cutlet.

"I'm sorry."

He shrugged. "What's for you to be sorry? You weren't even born."

The female volunteers ate lunch together in an empty dining hall. Yardena told them that the men would eat in the field. There were not enough members to take shifts tending the animals near the border.

On the way out, Yardena told Rebecca that she could join the gardening crew.

"Thank you," Rebecca said, wondering if she'd misjudged her.

"Don't thank me," Yardena said. "Shimon wants as many volunteers as possible clearing stones from the field. They want to plant next month."

The road reminded Rebecca of a quaint country lane. Clumps of bushes hugged the road, almost like hedges, and anemones threaded the winter green. Then, one after another, they passed two houses, their sides exploded outward, their concrete roofs lying intact on the ground. They didn't look as if they'd been blown up too long before.

"My parents would kill me if they knew I was up here," Rebecca overheard Eileen, a skinny dark girl from New Mexico, say to Sandy. "Their big worry is I'll marry some guy from a border settlement."

Sandy gave a snortly laugh. "If they saw these

guys, they wouldn't worry. 'Do you girls want to c-c-come to my r-r-room to l-l-listen to my Be-Be-Be-Be-Be-Be-Beatle records?. . . '"

Rebecca felt a coldness up her spine. Suddenly she understood the case of soda, the party that never happened. The man in blue stuttered.

Somehow she wasn't surprised.

The girls followed the tractor, pulling rocks from the loose earth and tossing them into the attached wagon. From the field they could see the border, a plain barbed-wire fence with wooden stakes on the other side of a ravine. Ron, the tractor driver, told them that the field had already been cleared twice before, but that it was still too rocky for planting. "The Syrians weren't interested in farming. For them it was just a mine field."

"Holy shit!" said Sandy. "And how are we supposed to tell the difference between a rock and a grenade?"

Ron smiled broadly, staring at Sandy's chest when he spoke. "If it blows up, it's a grenade."

On the way back from the field, Rebecca saw the man in blue next to the sheep shed. He slouched against the open gate, arms folded, waiting. A ragged line of sheep extended across the dirt road, into the surrounding field. Derek trailed behind the flock, a rifle under his arm.

Sandy gave a cat-call.

Derek replied with a wave of his rifle. "Wait a minute," he called out. "I'll walk back with you."

Rebecca dropped behind.

A few minutes later she was standing next to the water trough, ten feet behind the man, watching. The pen filled up quickly, even before all of the sheep had crossed the road. She didn't expect them all to fit, but they did.

With the last sheep in, the man closed the gate, picked up two buckets and approached the trough. Noticing Rebecca, he nodded.

"I didn't think they'd all get in," she said to him in Hebrew.

"G-Guess how many?" His eyes strained when he spoke.

"One hundred?" She said the first number that came to mind. Her attention was on the man's face, the tension in his jaw and neck.

"O-Over two hundred. You can't tell b-because they crowd together." He placed the buckets in the trough and turned on the water. "I could put in another fifty. W-Watch." He picked up a stone and threw it into the pen. The sheep scrambled in all directions, leaving a large empty circle where the stone had landed. "They're c-cowards, too," he added.

In the silence afterward, she watched the gradual spread of fur, like a swelling sponge, until the space no longer existed.

"And you were c-clearing the field?"

Nodding, she looked down at her hands. They were caked with dirt, except for the knuckles, which were scraped and raw.

"It's a shitty job." He removed the buckets and set them down on the ground. "P-Put your hands in the water."

She placed her hands under the tap and rubbed them together. Her knuckles began to bleed.

"Never mind. In a c-couple days, they'll be hard. M-Mine used to be like that too." He spread his hands. She had the urge to touch the thickened palms and say, "You don't have to speak. You know that rap on the window? It was me." Instead she wiped her hands on her pants and said, "You're not from a kibbutz or *moshav?*"

"I'm from Haifa. Th-Three generations. My mother wouldn't even let us have a dog." He grinned. "And now I'm a shepherd. L-Like an Arab." He picked up the two buckets and carried them back to the sheep pen. Rebecca followed. At the pen, he pointed his jaw at the gate, and she opened it. He poured the water into the metal trench.

"Yossi!" a voice called out.

Rebecca turned. The Arab from last night was hurrying toward them.

"Our Druze guard," Yossi said to Rebecca. "He's worth t-ten soldiers."

The old man slapped Yossi on the back. "*Nu?* The baby's coming," he said. "The water? Psssh!" To Rebecca, he held up two hands. "I have ten. Two dead."

She couldn't tell if he recognized her or not.

Outside the dining hall, on a metal folding chair, sat Rahel. Her hands were folded high on her belly, and her legs were slightly apart. Everyone crowded around her, laughing and joking. Yossi broke into the circle. Rebecca followed.

When Rahel saw Yossi, she removed one hand from her belly and reached for him.

"I-It hurts?" he asked, taking her hand and squeezing.

"Not so bad."

"Where's Shimon?"

She gestured toward the dining hall. "He's going over the housing plans with Ron for the meeting tonight. He doesn't change, does he, Yossi?"

As if in reply, he stroked her hair. Her temples were beaded with sweat.

Rahel smiled up at Rebecca. "A sweetheart, no?"

A few seconds later, Shimon hurried toward Rahel, Ron at his side. "Don't let those religious fanatics fuck us," he was shouting. "No changes in these plans, you understand?" He pushed a roll of blueprints at him.

Ron tucked the roll under his arm, grinning. "Don't worry. You take care of your own business."

Shimon turned to Rahel, picked up the plastic suitcase next to her, and extended an arm. "*Nu*, my wife?"

She took his hand and strained up out of the chair.

"I'll drive you," said Yossi.

"You crazy?" Shimon said. "I want everyone at that meeting."

As the tender pulled away, Shimon tooted his horn and flashed a V sign out the window.

Rahel, looking suddenly small and childlike in the front seat, waved.

Turning to Rebecca, Yossi said, "Do you want to c-come to the meeting tonight?"

The meeting, she learned on the drive over to the neighboring settlement, was about the new housing. To save on costs, the two settlements had decided to build together, only they couldn't agree on housing plans. Nefesh HaGolan wanted to start off with two rooms, the other settlement three.

The members of Nefesh HaGolan sat together in a clump on the dining hall floor. Looking around, Rebecca realized that these other settlers were religious couples with babies. There were even a few older children of maybe four or five. They scooted in and out of the kitchen on tricycles, their little plaid skullcaps held on by bobby pins.

In the shouting match that followed, Ron was the spokesman for Nefesh HaGolan. Each time one of the men from the other settlement complained about the lack of a second bedroom, Ron shouted back, "Your sex life is your own problem. We have a budget."

And so it went on all night, back and forth.

Yossi sat quietly, smoking. Every now and then he glanced at his watch.

"Do you think the baby's born yet?" Rebecca finally asked.

He shrugged. "Rahel is always a bit of a rascal. In the army she u-used to drive Shimon crazy." Smiling, he added, "He was her drill sergeant."

"You were in the army together?"

"They're the r-reason I'm here. The whole settlement is Shimon's dream. He'd do a-anything to get it built, e-even this." He tipped his chin at a child with shoulder-length ringlets riding a tricycle. Despite the hair, Rebecca knew it was a boy who had not yet reached the age for his first haircut.

By ten o'clock, the smoke was so thick that Rebecca's eyes burned. Most of the children were asleep, in arms and carriages, but none of the mothers had budged.

Checking his watch again, Yossi said to Rebecca, "It'll be o-over soon."

She nodded, unsure whether he meant the meeting or the birth.

"What we need is a party," Ron shouted on the ride home. "A celebration." He was sitting on a bale of hay in the back of the open lorry. "American woman. . ." he sang, snapping his fingers. "Rebecca. Where's your pretty friend? You should have brought her along."

She leaned back against Yossi, not bothering to answer.

He slipped an arm around her waist.

As they pulled to a halt in the dirt lot, Yardena emerged from the hut. She had stayed in the office to answer the telephone.

"Twice Shimon called to see if you're back," she said, arms folded against her chest. "Rahel's still in labor."

Ron jumped off the lorry. "Yardena. Call the girls. We're going to have a party."

"It's after eleven. They're sleeping."

"Wake them! We can't have a party with two girls."

Yardena's gaze shifted to Rebecca, standing next to Yossi. "One girl," she said, and walked off. But after ten feet she pivoted around. "A girl your age should have more sense."

For the next hour or so the three of them hung around the office waiting for Shimon's call. When, around midnight, he still hadn't telephoned, Ron said to Yossi, "Go on," and pointed with his cigarette at the door.

Rebecca noticed the look that passed between the two men.

Then Yossi stubbed out his cigarette, stood up, and held out his hand to Rebecca.

In his room, he put on his stack of forty-fives and offered her an orange soda. For a while she stood at the window, looking out, imagining herself looking in.

Then he turned out the light.

Even after he fell off to sleep, she lay awake. With her right hand, she kept lifting the stack of records, playing them over and over.

She heard the door open and looked up. At first she mistook the bulky figure for Ron. Then she recognized the thick, wiry hair.

"Yossi!" Shimon stood over them, peering down. She couldn't tell if he saw her. "Yossi." Shimon sank down on the bed.

"Shimon?" Rebecca could feel the vibration in Yossi's chest.

"The baby died, Yossele. Suffocated."

With two arms Yossi reached for Shimon and pulled him back onto the bed. Shimon's shoulder pressed against Rebecca's face.

Like a trespasser, she lay absolutely still, hiding in the warmth of their bodies.

5.
A MATTER OF TIME

Rebecca pushed through the flap of plastic that hung inside the doorway like lining in an old coat. Cigarette smoke and the smell of kerosene hit her. The cafe was smaller than she'd expected from the outside. More crowded, too. But all the customers, it seemed, were men. Drab, grey, distinctly European. It took her a moment to recognize Professor Frieling.

He was sitting at a table by a window, drinking brandy. A kerosene heater burned near his feet. Seeing her, he set down his glass and strained up out of his chair. By the time she crossed the room, he was standing. His wide-lapel jacket, the same one he lectured in, hung in loose folds. His pant cuffs bagged around the ankles. Even his hat fell over his eyes.

"My dear, my dear." Professor Frieling held out

his hand.

Reaching back, she couldn't tell if her hand was hot or his was cold. "Hi. I'm here. Am I late?"

He laughed, as if she'd said something wonderfully funny or clever, and motioned to her chair. "Please."

She sat, too quickly for him, and fought the impulse to jump up and start all over again. His fingers on the table edge trembled as he eased himself down.

Seated, he removed his hat. She was surprised to find his hair was gone, every bit of it. She'd never seen him without a hat before. Their classroom, a green cinderblock cell cut into the side of a Jerusalem wadi, was unheated.

After a moment's hesitation, he said, "I hope you don't think I'm in the habit of accosting every pretty young woman I meet."

"Oh no, I never thought that," she said, shaking her head. From the date under his name in their Hebrew poetry anthology she knew that he was older even than her own grandfather.

"God forbid, I'm not one of those. But I knew today was my last lecture and I wouldn't have another chance."

Her attention drifted back to his bald head. There was something odd about it. It took a few seconds to discover what. His scalp was firm and jellybean smooth, and so different from the loose crepe of his face that it looked as if a layer of skin had been peeled away.

"My dear, if my heart would and could still beat as when I was young, even two years ago, you would have heard it thumping when I listened to your wonderful presentation."

Startled, she stared at him. She wondered if she'd missed something. Yes, she'd given a ten-minute talk. All the Americans in the class had. But she didn't remember being particularly well-prepared.

"I am not flattering even myself," he continued, his eyes fastened on her, "when I say I scent genuine talent as naturally as I smell from afar the second-rate, not to say the fraudulent."

In the silence that followed Rebecca felt herself beaming, but couldn't stop. *Genuine talent.* It was the first time since she'd arrived here that someone told her she was special.

"The strange thing is Leni picked you out, too. 'Who's Oregon?' she asked after you all had gone."

He was referring to the party at his house. The invitation had taken the class of one-year students by surprise. Nothing seemed to lead up to it. Leni was an even bigger surprise. Tall, trim, white-haired, she wore dangling earrings and black silk slacks.

The only thing grandmotherly about her was the gold locket around her neck. Snapping it open, she leaned over to show Rebecca her grandchildren's baby pictures. "They're both in the army now," she said in an accent Rebecca couldn't place. "But I keep these pictures anyway. I think the face of anyone over two looks ridiculous in a locket, don't you?"

Later in the evening, Professor Frieling read one of his poems, something he had refused to do in class. Leni listened from behind his chair. It was a long poem, made longer by his line-by-line translation into English, and he kept coughing. Leni moved her hands from the velvet chair back to his shoulders. In the silence after he finished, she said, "Children, I don't want to be rude, but it's late and you really must go."

"It was such a cold miserable night," Professor Frieling was now saying. "And you were wearing sandals. Your legs were blue. I wanted to give you a pair of my socks." He paused, shrugging, his palms lifted. "But I feared you might think me the old fool."

The old fool. That was what he'd called himself this morning when he'd come up to her after class. "Would you care to meet this old fool for coffee?" She'd said yes, of course. Now she reached for his hands.

But somehow he ended up with his hands over

hers, his fingers around her wrists.

"Another brandy, Professor?"

He let go.

Looking up, Rebecca saw a spongy-haired Moroccan waiter in a white turtleneck and black bell-bottomed trousers. He had a deep tuck in one corner of his mouth, as if he might break out laughing.

Professor Frieling covered his glass. "Leni won't let me out again," he joked in Hebrew.

"Some things a wife should stay out of," the waiter replied with a wink at Rebecca.

She barely noticed. She was peering through the cigarette haze at the whiskey bottles in the little wooden nooks behind the bar. She hadn't had hard liquor since her duty-free bottle of scotch ran out.

"Nu?" The waiter tapped his foot.

"Cappuccino," she said.

"And Shlomo," Professor Frieling called out as the waiter was about to turn away. "Please bring my young friend three Suchard chocolate bars with cherry filling."

"But I'll never be able to eat three," Rebecca interrupted in English.

"Then take them home with you, my dear. I've yet to meet a young woman who doesn't love chocolate and cherries."

"So tell me a story, Rebecca," he said.

She looked up from the chocolate. She was having a hard time eating it. The bar was too hard to bite into. And when she tried to break it, it shattered.

"A story?"

"About yourself. Why you came," he said, straining forward.

"You mean you don't want the truth?"

He laughed. A whitish spittle pushed its way into the corners of his mouth. It reminded her of the juice of the milkweed plant she used to play with in the drying fields behind her house.

"I want nothing more. But truth takes so much time. . . "

"I'm in no hurry," she replied, smiling back.

He reached up and wiped his mouth. "But I promised Leni I'd be home by five."

She began with the story Michael hadn't wanted to hear, about her grandfather and the peddler's wagon, wheels missing, weathered boards as smooth as glass. "It was located behind the brick warehouse in a dirt lot with broken glass and rusted bits of metal that got all lush and weedy in summer. I remember one afternoon when the goldenrod and nettles were so high that the wagon seemed to be floating. My grandfather lifted me up over the rim and told me that when he was very young, before there was ever a store, he used to travel around in the wagon with his own father, my great-grandfather . . . "

But the story she ended up dwelling on was one she hadn't even known she remembered. "One time my grandfather took me to a party, just the two of us. I suddenly found myself sitting at a long table with a bunch of kids I'd never seen before. They were waving flags and eating cake. Finally, my grandfather came back to me again, and stuck a little pin into my dress. 'It's Israel's tenth birthday.' I looked around the table again, wondering which of the kids was Israel, why he had such a funny name. If maybe that was the reason he didn't want us to know who he was."

Professor Frieling leaned forward.

"Afterwards, I put the pin in my jewelry box, the kind every little girl had, make-believe leather with fake gold tooling. For years, whenever I looked at it I got the funniest feeling inside. Almost like a reminder of something, but I didn't know what."

Professor Frieling placed his hand around her wrist and squeezed. "For your sake, certainly not mine, I wish you'd been like every other child and thrown your pin away."

She looked up, startled. It was not the response she had expected. Or wanted.

"You're not happy here. I could hear your disappointment that day in class."

Again she wondered about what she could have revealed in those ten minutes. "It's true, it's not what I expected. . . " she began and broke off. She was looking for the right words to tell Professor Frieling that she no longer thought of happiness the way she had when she first came here: as something tangible she could inspect and measure at the end of each day, and feel guilty about if it fell short.

But by the time she was ready to speak, he was already in mid-sentence. ". . . the sad truth is that had I known fifty years ago what I know today, I would have tucked myself away in an Indian village in your wonderful American Northwest, not have raised a family, not written a line of my own, and nobody would have known where I got lost."

The rest of their hour together Professor Frieling talked. She listened. A couple of the stories he told were about people she knew from books; most of them she had never heard of. One man, a musician with a red beret, was actually in the cafe, seated around a large round table with a bunch of other old men. "A fraud right down to his toes," Professor Frieling said, leaning forward on his elbows. "Though Leni would never admit it. She has a weakness for that sort."

Rebecca turned again and stared. She wanted to fix every detail in her mind.

When she got home, she put the remaining two chocolate bars in an empty tin of Dutch butter cookies she had splurged on in a grocery that sold imported goods in the Old City. Even though she wasn't all that keen on chocolate, each night before she went to bed, she would cut a thick slice of bread from the loaf she kept in her bedroom cupboard, put a few shards of chocolate on it, and place the slice on the tile floor, under the coils of her electric heater. Afterward, eating the melted chocolate slice, warming her bottom on the still-hot tiles (Mrs Bozo only allowed her to use the heater five minutes morning and evening), she would think about stories to tell Professor Frieling on Thursday, the day they had decided to meet regularly.

That week she also took out a volume of Professor Frieling's poetry from the library, and spent hours looking up words in her dictionary.

The following Thursday it was very warm. The cafe garden was packed, and not just with the usual

old men, but with tourists, too, attracted no doubt
by the miniature Israeli flags stuck into the Campari
umbrella tops. Rebecca peeked through a gap in
the canvas sheeting. She saw the fraud in the red
beret, but not Professor Frieling.

But at least the front door was wide open, the
flap of plastic clipped to one side, the heaters off.
There weren't even enough men in the room to
stain the air with cigarette smoke.

This week she had no trouble spotting him. He
was the only one wearing a hat. She wondered how
he could be cold on a day like today — if perhaps he
had some sort of circulation problem.

Waving, she strode toward him. He couldn't
stand fast enough and she reached the table before
he'd straightened up.

She watched, her hand extended to help.

"My dear," he said, clasping her arm below the
elbow. "You're even five minutes early."

She smiled. "I walked. It took less time than I
thought."

"I hope you'll forgive me." He gestured to the
dim room. "You'd probably prefer to sit outside."

She shook her head. "It's too crowded out there
anyway."

This time she matched her pace to his, and they
both reached their seats at the same time. When

she saw him removing his hat, she was about to say, "Please, leave it on." But there was something so startling, almost intimate, about his odd bald pate that she held off saying anything.

The waiter greeted Rebecca with a nod. He had beads of sweat over his upper lip, the same tuck in his mouth.

"Cappuccino, please," she said, no hesitation. She noticed that Professor Frieling had a glass of tea in front of him, a manila envelope underneath his baggy jacket sleeve.

"And chocolate?" the waiter asked with arched eyebrows.

"Of course," Professor Frieling answered for her. "Three, same as last week."

"And you, Professor? You sure you won't change your mind?" With a flick of the wrist, the waiter measured off the tiniest bit of air. When Professor Frieling said no, no brandy today, Shlomo winked. "Afraid of the wife, eh?"

This time Rebecca caught the gesture. As soon as the waiter was gone, she said, "I liked Leni. And you can tell she cares so much for you."

"Yes, she fusses with me, if that's what you mean."

She thought back to the night of the party. "I

mean she cares."

Professor Frieling placed two fingers against the bridge of his nose, and closed his eyes. When he opened them, he said, "Her lovers have all thrown her over. And there's nothing she can do about it. Sometimes, I even feel sorry for her. I see her taking such pains with her toilette." He leaned forward. "She's sunk so low that she's even trying to attract me again."

Rebecca reddened and looked away. She could feel him peering at her, as if he expected her to say something. But she had nothing to say, so their silence continued until the waiter arrived with their order. "One. Two. Three." With a flourish, Shlomo stacked up the chocolate bars in front of her.

Almost immediately, Professor Frieling began to tell her about a friend of his in Poland in the 1920s, a would-be poet like himself, but more handsome. "One peasant woman, a charwoman, used to call him 'the young Jesus,' and cross herself whenever she passed him." The two young men had come to Palestine together. But five weeks later, his friend was dead. Malaria.

As soon as Rebecca saw Professor Frieling reaching for the manila envelope she had noticed, she knew what was inside. She watched him fumble with the clasp.

"I came across these poems while I was doing my own much belated-housekeeping. They're really not bad. One is even good. I'd forgotten completely I had them. At first glance I mistook them for my own."

He withdrew from the envelope a thin sheaf of crisp, white paper and placed the poems between them.

"Try your hand at translating them, my dear," he said. "I know an American journal that would publish them."

She stared. "They're in very good condition," she said at last, looking up.

"Of course," he went on, smiling. "They've just been retyped."

She looked down again. She couldn't say exactly why, but she suddenly distrusted him.

"Don't be afraid, Rebecca. You shouldn't be." His voice was soft, coaxing. "I know what you can do."

"How?" She gave him a point-blank stare. "You've read nothing I've ever written."

"I told you already. I have a nose for the first-rate." He nudged the pile. The top sheet slid off. "I'll help you. We'll do it together. We can start right now, or tomorrow."

"Why don't you just do it yourself? You don't

need me, you know that." The words came out more sharply than she had meant them to.

There was a silence.

A slant of light from the window was hitting her in the eyes. She couldn't see Professor Frieling, only lines radiating from a shiny disk. But again she was aware of him looking at her. The muscles in her face tightened. Her breathing slowed. It was the remembered sensation of pretending to be asleep, the fear that at any moment she would lose control.

"You have lovely skin," she finally heard him say, his fingers grazing her cheek. "You can always tell the true quality of a woman's skin when she sits in sunlight."

That week she didn't stash her chocolate bars in the cookie tin. She gave them to Mrs Bozo. The books she returned to the library. She even stopped applying blusher to her cheeks.

Thursday morning she made up her mind not to show up at the cafe. He could just sit and wait. But by 3:30 she couldn't keep her eyes off the clock. Even the Yemenite student sharing her cafeteria table noticed.

"If you're going somewhere, you should leave early," he said in Hebrew. "The buses will be terrible because of all the talk of snow."

Rebecca insisted she was going nowhere.

But five minutes later she got up abruptly and hurried out.

At the bus, everyone was bunched around the doorway, and by the time she gained a foothold, the driver was trying to close the door. Instead of stepping down, she wedged herself in until he relented.

"Ah, *ha'amerika'it*." No sooner had she pushed aside the plastic flap than Shlomo was beside her, a tray of dirty dishes resting on his shoulder.

"He's not here," she said, out of breath, staring at the empty table next to the window.

"He didn't know how to get in touch with you. He told me to tell you he can't come. He's sick."

She nodded, and turned to go.

He caught her by the arm. "Why not go to his house?"

It was his tone, the urgency of his touch, that told her that Professor Frieling was very sick. "He said I should?"

There was a pause. The tuck in the waiter's mouth deepened. "Professor Frieling is a *gentleman*." He said "gentleman" in English. "Wait a second." The tray still balanced on his shoulder, he reached

underneath the counter and came out with a Suchard chocolate bar. "For the wife."

Rebecca dug into her purse for money. But
Shlomo clicked his tongue. "Nonsense," he said.
"They've been hanging around for ages. No one
else buys them."

Rebecca pressed the buzzer.

Leni answered. "Oh, Oregon," she said, tucking
some stray hairs behind her ear. She had on a
flowered house dress and fake fur slippers, no make-
up. The house smelled of kerosene, and something
else. Mint, maybe?

"I came to see Professor Frieling, I mean if it's all
right."

Leni swung open the door. "Look at you," she
said, shaking her head. "Where do you think you
are? Miami?"

Rebecca looked down. As usual, she had no socks
on. "It doesn't bother me," she said.

"No, but you should really learn to take better
care of yourself. You won't always be young."

Rebecca looked up and their eyes met.

"Oh, I almost forgot." Rebecca handed her the
chocolate bar.

Leni turned it over in her hands. "My mother used
to say, 'His whole life a man puts on his pants the

same way.'" Then she handed it back.

Rebecca blushed. She should have realized there had been others before her.

Leni touched her elbow. "Never mind. I have a touch of diabetes, and the less sugar I eat the better."

Bracing herself, Rebecca stepped into the room Leni had pointed to. She remembered it as his study, and was surprised when she saw him in bed. Then she vaguely recalled a couch against a wall of books.

He laughed. "I was afraid to hope."

He was sitting up. Pillows protruded at odd angles behind his back. A blue knitted cap, the kind she'd seen only Arab laborers wear, sat crooked on his head. A pile of papers was on the foot of his bed, and at least a dozen more on the floor.

"Hi," she said, softening.

"The old fool, huh?" He patted his cap. "My only consolation is that a toupee would look even more foolish."

Smiling, she picked her way to his bed past the piles on the floor. But when he clamped on to her arm, she made an exaggerated display of looking around for a place to sit. The only chair was his desk chair, and that, too, had a stack of papers on it.

"Throw it on the floor," he said, letting go. "I can do without another reminder of all the things I've started and never finished."

She crouched down instead. That's when she realized she was still holding the chocolate bar. "Shlomo gave it to me, for your wife. I guess he didn't know she wasn't supposed to have sugar." She put the candy down on the dusty mahogany table, next to a glass of mint tea and some photographs.

"Don't be silly," he said and laughed. "Eat it. Please. It's how I always think of you."

"I really don't feel like it," she murmured.

In the long silence that followed, she stared at the photographs on the table. She recognized the grandchildren in their army uniforms. She also recognized Professor Frieling with his two little girls at the beach. She knew it was he because of the thick hair and the way he held his girls, by their wrists, as the three ran toward the camera.

She could feel Professor Frieling looking at her, waiting.

She began to talk about the snow. "I'd love to see Jerusalem in a snowstorm. I was sure I wouldn't get to. I mean, who would expect it to snow so late?"

He didn't answer.

She listened to his scratchy breathing. "Do you want your tea?" she finally said. "I think it's still hot. Or I could make you a new glass."

He shook his head. His fingers, she noticed, were

clasping the bunched-up sheet. His knuckles were white.

She looked away, to the neat stacks on the floor. There were dozens of manila envelopes.

"It's all Leni's doing," he suddenly burst out. "Fussing around, making piles, moving them. I don't know if she does it to torture me or if sexless old age has sparked her nesting instinct." His voice was hard and angry, and touched her to the quick. She knew it was she, and not Leni, who was the real source of his rage.

"You should probably go," he said. "You'll get caught in the snow."

She stood up but made no motion to put her coat on. She felt suddenly close to him, as if their disappointment and anger with each other had finally forged some sort of meeting ground. "I'll come back if you want," she said.

He shuddered. The sticky white corners of his mouth turned down. "Even an old fool has his self-respect."

She intended to kiss his cheek, but he lifted his head off the pillow and pushed his mouth at her. She forced herself to stay absolutely still.

But she didn't fool him.

Sinking back onto the pillow, he turned his head away and squeezed his eyes shut.

She tried to think of something to say, but all she could come up with were things like "I'm sorry" and "It's okay". So in the end she just said "Good-bye" and left.

In the hallway, she heard a clacking and caught a glimpse of Leni at the kitchen table, her fingers pecking away at a typewriter keyboard. She tiptoed to the front door.

The street lamps were already on. The wind had picked up. And a few isolated flurries, as feathery as milkweed tufts, hovered in the band of light.

6.
THE WEDDING

"*Rega. Rega.*" Rebecca ran after the Haifa bus, arms waving, as it rolled out of the station bay. Avner stood on the last step, wedged into the doorway, and when Rebecca got close enough, he grabbed her arm and hauled her up.

"*Amerika'it!*" an old woman shook her fist at Rebecca as she stumbled after Avner to the back of the bus. "This is no 'special'. You want a taxi? Go across the street and pay for one."

Rebecca slid into the seat next to Avner. "Damn the old witch!"

"Don't take it into your heart," he said, smiling sideways.

She nodded, out of breath, and looked Avner over. For the wedding, he was wearing a white nylon shirt and shiny navy-blue dress slacks. She wondered if her dress was okay. It was the first dress she'd ever bought in Israel, and when she told the sales-woman it was for a Yemenite wedding, the woman tossed in two detachable sleeves in the same flowery cotton. Rebecca hadn't sewn them in, she hadn't had time, but they were tucked inside her pocketbook along with her toothbrush, panties, and miniature sewing kit. Just in case.

"I'm sorry that I'm late . . . " she began in her stilted, formal Hebrew.

Avner listened, eyes coaxing her on. Unlike most Israeli students who insisted on answering her in English, Avner would answer her in whatever language she addressed him. She liked that about him: the way he followed a conversation, neither pushing nor hanging back, but always ready for the unexpected turn.

"Never mind," he said when she finished. "As long as you came." He wiped his dark shiny fore-head with the back of his hand. Although it was only May, summer had already burned away spring, sapping the honeysuckle from the air. "I thought maybe you changed your mind," he added.

In English, she said, "You don't really think I'd do that, do you? Just not show up?"

"No. But when I asked you to come you sounded so . . ." He pressed his thumb and forefinger to-gether, as if he were taking a pinch of salt. "So not comfortable. Like a girl who doesn't want to dance with you but doesn't know how to say no."

She looked into his face. It was a handsome face — Yemenite Jews are handsome people — but she could imagine girls turning away. Middle-class Ashkenazi girls did not date Yemenite boys from poor farm villages.

"If I didn't want to dance with you, I'd know how to say no." The words out, she blushed. They had never flirted before. Their words, across a library table, or over a cup of coffee, had been tentative, spare, to the point. That was why she was so surprised when, yesterday, he asked her to the wedding. "The truth is I didn't have a dress to wear."

Avner looked down at her flouncy new dress and smiled. "Very pretty, but I'm sorry you bought it special. Why not the one like this?" He sliced a line across his thighs.

"My mini?" She wrinkled up her face. "But you told me your family is religious."

"I also told you my father, he goes without shoes all the time. Maybe you, too, want to try?"

Rebecca caught the flirtatious tone in his voice, an echo of her own.

"Besides." He grew suddenly serious. "I didn't think Americans worried about things like that. That's what's so wonderful about them. They do what they want and don't care what anybody thinks."

"Says who?"

Avner touched her chin. "You, Rebecca. You tell me this all the time."

Avner gestured to his red plastic suitcase on the sandy shoulder of the one-lane road where the bus had dropped them. She should sit down. It might be a while before they got a lift into the *moshav*. Few outsiders would be coming to the wedding, and it was too late for ordinary traffic.

She looked at Avner's suitcase and cursed herself for not bringing along even a knapsack. What would the people in his village think of an *amerika'it* who came to spend the night with only a toothbrush and panties in her pocketbook?

"Can't we walk?" she asked, casting her eyes over the orange groves that swallowed up the road into the village. The sun had already dropped behind the trees, turning the leaves a shimmery black.

He looked down at her sandaled feet.

She wriggled her toes at him.

Laughing, he picked up his suitcase with one hand and took her hand with the other. Neither of them spoke.

"I'm happy you came. That I asked you," he said

at last, their clasped hands swinging as they fell into step.

Rebecca breathed in the orangey smell that seemed to thicken with the growing darkness. "Is it a good friend who's getting married?" she asked.

"Benny and I, we were like brothers growing up. After the army, we both left Nativ. I to university. He abroad."

"America?"

"Sweden. Always, from the time we were children, he swore that after the army he'd leave the *moshav* and go enjoying life."

"And you?"

"You know, Rebecca, I am the youngest of eight children. Seven girls. When I'm born, it's like I'm the *mashiach* himself. To make me my mother does everything: even go to an old witch who gives her garlic and charms and who knows what else to put under her pillow. My father, he prays all day." He chuckled. "I'll tell you a story. The first thing I remember is my mother running after me with a red ribbon she wants to tie back on my hand so the evil eye won't get me. But I run faster, I hate the red ribbon, and then I trip and cut open my head. She cries and I have so bad feelings I promise her always I'll wear the red ribbon." He halted and regarded their clasped hands. "So you see it's not so easy for me to go. Even to go to university was hard. I'm the first from my village."

"But at least you don't wear a red ribbon." She looked up, head tilted, eyebrows raised. "Or is there something you haven't told me?"

He met her gaze. "Some things you have to find out for yourself."

Her cheeks burned. "You've never given me the chance." She'd known Israelis who asked for a date in less time than it took her to sign the back of a check, and yet Avner had sat across from her for months and never hinted at anything. Even now, she felt sure she'd been more aware of him, his body and how he moved and breathed, than he had been of her.

At that moment a white pickup truck packed with people overtook them and rattled to a stop. But Avner waved it on. Peering at the receding faces, dark, smooth-skinned, even-featured, she could almost believe they came from a single mold.

"That first day I spoke to you in the cafeteria was not the first time I saw you," he said as the truck disappeared from sight.

She found herself smiling.

"In the summer I was a guard on weekends in your dormitory. I even helped you that first night with your suitcase."

She pulled up short. "That I don't believe!"

"You arrived on a Friday afternoon."

She struggled to locate his face behind some stubborn flap of grey matter, but in vain. "But I had no idea."

He shrugged. "So how you want me to give you the chance if you didn't even know I exist?"

The village at dusk reminded her of a hastily-built, unfinished stage set: tacked onto the original prefab bungalows were crude additions, all in various stages of construction. Even the one road, empty save for a few chickens, appeared to drop off abruptly after the last house.

"I guess we're late," she said.

He pointed with his chin down the road. Her eyes followed the imaginary line until she made out a soft orb of light. But almost immediately the circle dissolved into tiny pinpricks that got brighter and brighter. Coming towards them, she realized, was a cluster of men, maybe fifteen or twenty, their faces illumined by candles. For some moments they seemed to be floating. Then they materialized, old men mostly, with embroidered skullcaps and white ear locks and baggy pants. But also a few younger men like Avner — slim, smooth-shaven, in white nylon dress shirts. In the middle, pressed upon by all sides, was the bridegroom. He was the only one wearing a suit, and he looked as if his tie was choking him.

Avner led Rebecca to the side of the road as the procession approached. Now she could see that two old men were actually leading the bridegroom, their hands gripping high under his arms. When the bridegroom saw Avner, he made a movement with his shoulders, almost like a shrug, and for a moment the men lost their grasp. But within seconds everything was as it was before.

"But your friend came back after all."

Avner nodded. "Less than a year he was away."

"What happened?"

Avner lifted Rebecca's hand, turned it over and rubbed the palm. "How old are you?"

"Twenty-one."

"And how many places you lived in your twenty-one years?"

She flexed her outstretched fingers. "Including Israel?"

"Including."

"Five. No six."

"You see this village? It was the same village in Yemen, same families even, just picked up and put down here. And to our village in Yemen the people came after the destruction of the Temple. So for your six places in twenty-one years, we have one place in two thousand."

"Your friend doesn't look too happy."

"He's embarrassed."

"Because he came back?"

"Because always he said he'd marry a Swedish girl with long, blond hair." Avner broke into a grin. "The bride is my little cousin."

She swallowed. "Does he love her?"

"Love?" He looked into her eyes. "If the men married for love, our village wouldn't stay together two thousand years."

"And the women?"

"The Yemenite women love to be married. That's the only love they know."

She thought of the sleeves in her pocketbook. "You mean they're virgins when they marry."

He hesitated. "That's not what I meant. But yes, they are."

They continued down the street in silence, feet crunching on the unpaved road.

"I must leave my suitcase at my parents," he said as they cut across a dirt lot. "My father will be home. His legs are not good. He doesn't go out any more."

The house was at the end of the street, not fifty meters from a barbed-wire fence that Avner told her was the old '67 border. It was one of the few houses that didn't have an addition. Through the open window, Rebecca saw an old man with long white ear locks and an eastern skullcap lying on a quilted bed. Bare feet stuck out of his pantlegs. His hands gripped a black book. But his head was tilted, as if he were listening.

"I didn't bring a suitcase," she blurted out.

"Never mind."

"In America we like to travel light." She shook her pocketbook.

"It's not important."

"I think I'll wait outside."

He hesitated, then rested his bag on the stoop. "Later, we'll go in. Come. I hear the women. You can get a look at your bride and decide for yourself if she is in love."

In the distance she heard what she took for a high-pitched wind instrument, and soon she caught sight of another procession, similar to the first, but composed of women and girls. The dresses of the older women were black, the bodices heavy with gold filigree, but the dresses of the girls were like her own, full and flowery, barely reaching the knee. The noise, she realized, was coming from the older women, who vibrated their fingers against the in-sides of their mouths. Together, the girls and women showered the bride with hard candies.

The bride was a skinny girl of maybe seventeen, with kohl-lined eyes and a red mouth. Her wedding gown of gold brocade looked as if it might weigh more than she did. To add to the weight, her hair was covered in a cone-shaped headdress of silver and gold mesh, her arms looped with bracelets. Instead of a bouquet, a thick band of roses and chrysanthemums was woven into the headdress. Yet the girl bobbed along, giggling and waving, eyes flashing, certainly in no need of anyone to hold her up.

Avner slipped out of the shadows of the orchard and waved to a tiny woman with wide wrinkles, bad teeth, and a quick step, dancing along next to the bride. The woman tossed a handful of candies at Avner, who caught two or three, then tossed them on to Rebecca. The woman's eyes followed the candy from Avner to Rebecca, still in the shadows. Rebecca clutched the candy against her chest and smiled. The woman stared, lost a step, then took a running leap to catch up.

The procession gone, Avner said, "My mother wants me to get married."

She handed him one of the candies. "Anyone in particular?"

"The village girls are all alike." His fingers played

with the paper wrapping. "When I finish my studies next month I'm to return here to be a teacher."

"I think they're very beautiful. They remind me of girls in the Bible. The kind that fathers sent their servants out looking for."

"Sent their *servants* out looking for?" She could hear the hard edge to his voice. "I thought you were the one who asked me about love?"

"And you told me it had no place here." Rebecca closed her eyes and breathed deep the sticky night scent of oranges.

"For other men."

"And for you?" She could feel her heart.

"You know, Rebecca. All year I watch you, like the moth watching the fire, coming closer and closer. In the combat I wasn't afraid. Maybe because I have not the time. But with you I'm afraid."

She opened her eyes. "Ah. A woman of ill-repute. Is that what you're afraid of?" She opened her purse and whipped out the detachable sleeves she'd stuffed inside along with the sewing kit, toothbrush, and panties. "Do you think if I sewed them in I'd pass for a virgin?" she said, dangling them in front of her.

Avner took the sleeves from her. "A woman who plays games. All year I watch you, and always you're different. Even today, when I see you running for the bus, I almost don't know you in this dress."

"I used to know exactly who I was, even when my friends didn't. But being here's done funny things to me." She tugged at a leafy citrus branch, then let it snap back. "You heard that old lady on the bus. *Amerika'it*. And here I'd just bought the same dress worn by half the girls in Jerusalem."

"But why you want to fit in? Why can't you say 'Fuck you, Israelis. This is me'?"

Rebecca hesitated, surprised. Avner had never spoken like this before. "Why can't you?"

He looked up.

"You can't even think of not coming back to your village."

He rested his hands on her waist. "Who says I don't think?"

She watched his Adam's apple as he spoke.

"You know, Rebecca, our Hebrew has not the swear words. Not one. If we want to say 'fuck you,' we must say it in English or Arabic. I believe it's not a coincidence. We Israelis talk all the time about breaking away, cutting loose, leaving the society. But it's hot air. Even the language doesn't let us. For a Yemenite it's a hundred times worse. Look at Benny."

"You know English and Arabic, and you said it just fine."

Avner drew her to him. "It's not the same thing.

If a man is finally to say it, he must to find the way
to say it in his own tongue."

She knew he was about to kiss her and she
reached up to meet him.

"Come. I'm in the mood for a wedding."

Avner led her down the road until they reached
a cluster of animal pens and farm sheds. Strings
of colored lights crisscrossed the dirt stockade
adjacent to the barn. Rows of long, narrow tables
and benches ringed the stockade from the outside. The entire village was gathered here, laughing
and shouting, showing off babies, paying no attention to the wedding ceremony taking place off
in one corner. Avner introduced her to everyone
they bumped into. The noise was so loud she didn't
have to worry about talking or making herself
understood.

At the bridal meal, she found herself squeezed
between two women with elaborate hair knots. Avner was nowhere in sight. A loudspeaker broadcast
what sounded like Arab music. The two women
hummed along. They were seated so close on the
bench that Rebecca couldn't turn to look at them,
but she could feel the rhythm of the music through
their shoulders. Before long, tin bowls, the kind she
had seen only in old war movies, were passed

around and a curry smell filled the air. Suddenly, she spotted Avner and his mother on the outskirts of the barn, just where the colored lights stopped. The old woman's mouth didn't stop moving, and every once in a while she rapped her forehead as if she was knocking on wood. Rebecca was so caught up in watching their pantomime that she didn't see the bowl of soup being passed to her and knocked it onto her lap.

The two women leaped up and began to scrape the lumps of potato off her. "It's okay," Rebecca said over and over, but the women refused to listen. The soup would stain, they told her, her pretty dress would be ruined. A little boy was dispatched to bring the "Johnson's," which she soon discovered was the baby powder.

"Enough, enough," she pleaded, as one woman held up the hem and the other attacked the stain. She knew that the imported powder cost a fortune and was reserved for newborns. By the time Avner appeared, a thick white paste covered the stain and the container was empty.

"So I see you decided to dress up a little more." He was smiling, but the muscles of his face were all wrong.

"It's such a waste. They used up the Johnson's." She clutched the empty container. "I couldn't stop them."

"You are a guest," he said.

"Your family is very nice. Your whole village. But I wish you hadn't left me alone."

"I had to speak to my mother." He looked away.

"Did I do something wrong?"

"My mother arranged for a cousin's granddaughter to come tonight."

She flushed. "Did you know before you asked me here?"

"A man knows and doesn't know. Every wedding and Bar-mitzvah and funeral, always she has someone picked out. Tonight is not the first time she believes the girl is the mother of her grandchildren."

"And she believes I'm the evil eye, is that it?" She tried to laugh, but her throat shut tight.

"She believes I'm the little boy who must to have a red ribbon. And she makes the show when I won't wear it."

"Maybe she's right. 'A woman who plays games.' You said so yourself."

"And if you are? A man must learn to make his own mistakes."

"I'm leaving in six weeks. I even have my ticket."

"Then we have not the minute to waste." He grabbed Rebecca's hand. "Maybe we won't have another chance to dance. Never."

She dug her heels into the dirt. "But nobody's dancing. Not a soul. And only a belly dancer could dance to that music."

"We'll be belly dancers together."

"Can't we wait till they play some pop music? You told me on the bus they'll play pop music after dinner."

He took hold of both her hands. "And you told me that if you didn't want to dance with me, you'd know how to say no."

"But why is this dance so important to you?"

"Yes or no, Rebecca?"

Hand in hand they made their way to the stockade. At first they just stood there, facing each other, stiff. Then Avner lifted his hands high over his head and began to rock his torso in rhythm with the music. Rebecca followed. Almost at the same moment their shoulders caught the beat, and then their hips, and they began to make loose circles around each other.

Suddenly, Rebecca couldn't tell if the musicians were playing louder or if the crowd was suddenly quiet. Fingers pointed. Heads poked into the spaces between the wooden railings. An old woman covered a little boy's eyes with her hand.

"Avner," she pleaded. "Please stop."

In reply, he let out a whoop, caught her up by the hips, and spun her.

The crowd blurred. The lights flew off their wire strings.

Rebecca closed her eyes and held her breath, braced for a fall.

7.
SANTA KATERINA

Rebecca crawled out of her sleeping bag, into the cold, night air, and slipped on Avner's floppy sandals. She snapped each foot, once, twice, to shake free the sand.

"What's the matter?" Avner murmured in Hebrew.

She listened to his deep, steady breathing. She liked to tell him that she fell in love with him because of the way he breathed, slowly, his shoulders rising and falling, his chest swelling, as if air were special and not to be wasted. In the library she would find herself staring at her book, listening. And after they became lovers, if a dream, a fear, jolted her awake, she had only to match her breaths to his and the panic would be gone. But tonight the even rhythms irritated her: maybe because the silence of the desert made all noise seem forced and unnatural. At one point, she had even nudged Avner awake.

But when he lifted his head, she felt selfish and child-ish, and pretended to be asleep.

"Nothing," she said at last. "I have to go to the bathroom."

"You want me to come?"

She stooped and kissed the top of his head. Sand from his hair stuck to her lips. "Go back to sleep."

She edged her way down the low shelf of rock, away from the moonlit ledge where everyone was sleeping. The soles of Avner's sandals crunched on the wadi bed. Through the dense blackness she couldn't make out the high canyon walls, just the connecting strip of starry sky. Her chest tightened. Her heart speeded up. She felt as if she were inside a box, a high box with holes punched in the cover, the kind that once upon a time she had kept frogs captive in. It was the identical feeling of claustro-phobia she had making camp this evening when, for no reason, she'd tripped and fallen on her wrist.

"Watch out for hyenas!" a voice rang out in the night.

She recognized Gideon's voice, his almost British English, and knew it was a joke. Yet her body let out a cry anyway.

Feeling silly and sheepish, she turned and waved in the direction of Gideon's voice.

"Hi!" she laughed, as if she had just spotted him

in a busy intersection.

But in truth she saw nothing at all.

"Coffee?" Gideon called out as she groped her way back to the ledge.

Looking up, she saw a flicker of light that hadn't been there before. He's sneaked off for a cigarette, she thought with a touch of glee, maybe because he'd made such a big deal of tossing away what were supposedly his last cigarettes as the jeep pulled out of Eilat.

Closer now, she realized her mistake. What she'd taken for a cigarette tip was a pilot light. Gideon was hunkered over the gas bubble, a blanket around his shoulders. The sand encrusted in his three-day stubble glittered in the reflected light.

"Coffee?" he repeated and smiled.

She peered up at the ledge. She could make out the gap between Tsipi and Doron, where Gideon should have been, as well as her own empty space to the right of the bump she knew was Avner.

"Sleeps like a baby," Gideon said, as if reading her mind.

She turned back to Gideon. His eyes were red and watery, and under each eye was a fleshy pouch rimmed with sand. "You've been up all night?" she asked.

"Like you."

She hesitated. She was never sure how to take Gideon's words. Especially the simple ones. Maybe because she'd made up her mind that first night he wasn't a simple man. Sometimes these three days she had the feeling he was speaking to her in code. That there was something he wanted to say to her. Or ask her.

"My wrist hurts," she mumbled. But when Gideon went on staring, she added, "Maybe it's also a little bit the desert. It's so black and quiet. And empty. There aren't even any smells. Nothing."

Gideon reached up and helped her down beside him. Then he handed her a corner of his blanket and a cup of Turkish coffee. She breathed the cardamon. The smell made up for the taste, which she didn't particularly like.

"Thanks." She felt a pang of remorse about the cigarettes.

"I was just kidding about the hyenas. I hope I didn't scare you."

She could feel him looking at her. She lifted her chin. She wondered if he'd heard her cry out. Or seen her startle.

Finally, Gideon leaned over and scooped up a handful of stones. "A couple years back in my class at the university I had an Arab boy from East Jerusalem," he said, sifting the stones through his thick fingers. "Very bright, but from a simple family. Afterward, I arranged for him to be assistant principal in a high school for boys in the Old City."

Rebecca sipped her coffee and listened. Around the campfire that first night, she'd had trouble following Gideon. He'd start a story that seemed to have nothing to do with whatever the rest of them had been talking about. And then, just when she was lost and about to give up, he'd say something that not only made the connection clear, but made anything anyone else had said seem superficial. Thinking about it afterward, she was happy that Avner had listened quietly, not trying to compete. Unlike Doron, who seemed even more stupid the harder he tried to impress.

"He told me that six years ago, when he was sixteen, his grandfather took him to the Jerusalem Zoo in the middle of the night. They got in by climbing over the fence. When they got to the hyena pen, the grandfather opened a sack of stones he had brought along and began to throw them at the animals."

"Real sweet game," she interrupted.

"It wasn't a game. In Arab superstition the hyena is an evil beast, almost like the devil. He counterfeits the laughter of men in order to trick them. The old man probably thought he was getting even for something. Who knows? A love affair, a bad business deal, maybe even for losing the war. Remember this is '67. In any case, by morning the hyena was dead."

"And your student threw stones, too?"

"I imagine so." He paused, fingering a stone. "Yes, certainly so. What's the point of the story, his telling me, if he didn't?"

Rebecca watched Gideon's thumb moving back and forth. "I'm not sure I understand the point," she said at last.

"Quite simple. Hate. What it means. . . "

"I mean of your telling me."

He smiled. "I thought it was the kind of story you'd like."

A moment passed. She looked him full in the face. "Sometimes I get the feeling that you *want* to scare me."

He lifted his eyebrows. "Do I?"

"Scare me?" She hesitated. "Sometimes."

"Then I'm sorry."

She gave him a point-blank stare. "Are you?"

He laughed. "Maybe not. But a person should know what he's getting into. Especially here."

"You think I'm not serious. That I'm a romantic *amerika'it*."

After a long silence, he said, "You know, Rebecca,

twelve years ago I left my wife and three children to marry Tsipi."

She nodded. She already knew this from Avner. This and Tsipi's many miscarriages.

"Maybe in America such things don't mean anything, but here in our Israel we take our families very seriously. So. . ." He spread his hands.

"So you were very much in love," she said, nodding again.

He dropped his hands to his knees. "Precisely."

"I'm afraid I don't follow," she said, shaking her head.

He picked up the finjon and refilled her cup, which she'd finished without knowing it. "Let's just say that while I was sitting here, watching you toss, I kept thinking, 'If I were twenty-one and free, I'd take the next plane out of here.'"

"Well, I'm not free," she said, forcing a laugh. "And I can't take the next plane."

A silence. She could feel him waiting.

"I ripped up my ticket," she finally said.

"Ah, so you really are scared."

Tsipi was the first to emerge from her sleeping bag. Leggy, no hips, clipped blond hair, in the dawn light she resembled a girl of fifteen. She even bounced as she followed the ledge down to the ravine. Rebecca suddenly wondered if Tsipi looked, walked, this way when Gideon married her. Or if, one by one, her miscarriages had whittled away whatever had been full and soft in her appearance.

Rebecca noticed that Gideon was also watching Tsipi. Arms folded, head back, he seemed to be daring her to look up. She didn't. Instead, the closer she got, the more intensely she scanned the wadi bed. Twice she stooped to examine a rock. One she discarded. The other she kept.

"Look at this," Tsipi said in Hebrew, squatting and opening her hand. Her palm stayed cupped.

Rebecca rolled onto her knees. "It's beautiful." The reddish nugget reminded her of an embryo.

Tsipi suddenly looked up. Instead of wrinkles, her face was threaded with minute capillaries. "Take it," she said, slipping the stone into Rebecca's hand. "I hope it brings you good luck here."

Gideon gave a quick laugh.

"Thank you," Rebecca said, closing her hand over the stone and getting up quickly. "I think I'll go unpack for breakfast."

One by one Rebecca placed the eggs in the pot of water. She couldn't get the conversation with Gideon out of her mind. Not so much the content as the rhythm. The winding stories that almost lost her. And then a word, a look, a pause. A connection. And then he was off again. Her head was spinning. She shouldn't have drunk all that Turkish coffee.

She started when she felt hands on her hips. "Jesus!" She whirled around, almost dropping the egg in her hand.

Avner stood barefoot and clean shaven, smelling all tangy.

"I hate people sneaking up on me," she said feebly.

"Someone stole my sandals."

In the silence that followed she felt him looking her over. Finally, he reached out and wrapped his fingers around her swollen wrist. "It hurts?"

"Just a *sprain*." She said 'sprain' in English, because she didn't know the Hebrew word.

"Try to squeeze the egg."

"I don't want to waste it."

"It'll be mine."

She squeezed until it cracked. "Now what?" she said, releasing her fingers.

He took the broken egg and emptied it into his mouth, grimacing as he swallowed.

"You didn't *have* to do that!" she burst out.

He looked into her face. "I keep my bargains."

She pondered him, the stickiness in the corner of his mouth, the shaving nick on his chin. "You should stop trying to shave," she said, reaching up and wiping away the egg.

"It reminds me of the army and funerals. It's a custom not to shave for thirty days after a death."

She returned to her cooking. "And I suppose you're going to tell me there's also a custom about eating raw eggs."

"When we were kids, we had a joke. You want an American egg? If you said yes, you got a raw egg. We got it from the cowboy movies."

Once, doubtful about some detail of American life he'd garnered from cowboy films, she pressed him for movie titles. "Titles?" he laughed. "You're talking about a bunch of dumb kids living in tin houses. We couldn't even read the Hebrew sub-titles. For us it was like cartoons."

"One day my father found me playing the joke on some friends," Avner went on. "He slapped my face."

"Just for that?"

"What if there was a blood spot, and I caused someone to eat it? You forget my father is a religious man."

"I forget nothing," she wanted to tell him, but a burst of laughter distracted her. Looking up, she saw Tsipi and Chana doubled over like schoolgirls. Next to them, bare-chested and hairy, in only his underwear, was Doron. He was singing as he shaved, every once in a while throwing in a little kick with his hairy leg. Rebecca recognized the tune from the campfires, a schmaltzy love song that he had embellished with all sorts of drawn-out chords on his guitar.

"Tell me he doesn't look like a dancing bear," Rebecca said.

Avner didn't answer.

She pressed on. "Don't you think it's strange that it's always the three of them together, and Gideon alone?"

This time Avner said: "In Israel, when people grow up together, they tend to stay together. Especially in the kibbutz."

When Avner had told her about the invitation she had assumed the third couple would also be Gideon's students. But Chana and Doron were childhood friends of Tsipi.

"And Tsipi doesn't even look at Gideon," she added, switching off the gas under the eggs. "It's as if she's guilty. Or afraid."

Avner crouched down, reached into the box of supplies, and came up with a loaf of bread and a knife.

"But she's always looking at Doron. And he's always looking at her. Sometimes I think that silly love song is meant for her." She paused, watching Avner slice the bread. He used the boulder as a cutting board. "Do you think they might be lovers?"

"I don't think," he said in a flat voice.

"That's not an answer." She drained off the water. "Last night Gideon hinted at problems."

"Yes, when people talk until dawn that's usually what they end up talking about."

Rebecca listened to the cutting sounds. "You were sleeping. Gideon couldn't sleep. Neither could I. I think he's very unhappy."

Avner's silence was like an accusation.

She swung around. "You know what I noticed? As soon as I bring up people or feelings, you have nothing to say. American eggs. Who gives a damn!"

He put down the knife. "Maybe you have enough to say for both of us."

Rebecca flushed. "You know what else Gideon said? If I had any sense, I'd leave."

She waited.

Avner reached inside the box for a tomato and began to cut it into tiny pieces.

After breakfast, they set off for Santa Katerina. With barely a word spoken, the group took up their usual positions in the jeep. Gideon sat up front next to Udi, their guide. Tsipi sat between Chana and

Doron on the second bench. Rebecca and Avner crouched in the crawl space in back. Gideon took out his bag of sunflower seeds and began to crack the seeds between his teeth. He'd purchased a kilo sack in Eilat to help him keep the "*regime*," as he called his plan to quit smoking. Since then, gusts of papery shells mixed with sand whipped periodically across the back seat.

Rebecca watched Avner as he bounced with closed eyes, pretending to be asleep. But he couldn't hide his bobbing Adam's apple, the tension around his mouth. She had the urge to slap him. *Look at me. Talk to me. What's happening to us? Why are we suddenly stepping all over each other? And why am I so scared?*

Before long the wadi broadened and flattened. For the first time in two days they passed goats, women in black, ragged-looking children. She had yet to see a man. She wondered where they were all hiding.

The jeep lurched to a stop not far from two boys of about fourteen, one with sneakers so big they slapped the sand as he walked, the other with rubber sandals. Both had cigarettes slanting down their chins.

"*Har Moshe*," Udi shouted, cutting the engine and pointing to a simple crest of red rock above a blur of green.

Rebecca raised her hand against the glare and peered. So this was Mount Sinai. It was certainly not what Charlton Heston had led her to expect.

Hearing a strange sound, she looked back at the jeep. Gideon had his head out the window and was making sucking noises at the two Bedouin boys. "Yes? *Cigaria?*"

The boys stared back, stony-faced.

Suddenly, the jeep sprang forward. From under his seat Gideon retrieved his bag of sunflower seeds.

Everyone waited in the jeep while Gideon entered Santa Katerina to present his letter from the Patriarchate in Jerusalem. He had been able to arrange private rooms in the monastery's guest wing, which was closed to the public, instead of in the group hostel.

When he returned a few minutes later, three Bedouin servants with white-wrapped heads followed. Two began to pull boxes and rucksacks from the jeep. The third motioned for them to follow him. They entered the yellow stone fortress single file, Gideon up front with the servant, Udi at the rear, the gun he always kept stashed under his front seat slung over his shoulder. They climbed a steep staircase. Through an arch on the first-floor landing, Rebecca saw a walled orchard with apple trees. She took a deep breath. But the trees had no smell, or none that carried into the monastery.

On the second floor, the servant led them down a corridor and into a reception room, then disappeared. They all began to wander around, touching the inlaid tables, the tapestry covers of the divans, the icons on the whitewashed walls. The room was clean and tidy, not a pillow out of place, not a speck of dust.

"Welcome." A black-frocked monk with a gappy beard carried in a brass tray with coffee. He motioned for them to sit. They did, stiffly. Whenever they moved, sand scattered from their clothing and hair. The monk smiled vaguely the entire time, but said nothing more. Rebecca wondered if there was some vow about silence.

When they finished their coffee, the same servant reappeared in the doorway and led them to their sleeping quarters: four private guest rooms off the third-floor balcony. Avner picked up their rucksacks stacked neatly along the outside corridor, and followed Rebecca into their room. It was cool and dim. Two narrow iron beds stood along opposite walls. A print of Jesus, his hands raised in benediction, was taped to the wall. He had a startled look on his face as if he'd just jumped backwards.

Rebecca crossed the stone floor to the small window, hoping to see the orchard below. But the walls were three feet thick and all she could see were the red hills they had just driven through.

"Rebecca."

She turned around. Avner was sitting on the bed, staring at the floor.

"You know," he began in English, "my parents speak to me in Arabic. I answer them in Hebrew. It doesn't make for communication. And growing up in my *moshav*, I'd speak with my friends only about soccer, the army, girls maybe. But not about books, or ideas, or the feelings. When I went away to university, I was even more the stranger." He looked up. "For the first year I don't think I opened my mouth in class. Ask Gideon."

She crossed the room and sat down next to him. "But next year you'll be his research assistant. And he invited us on this trip," she added, placing her hand on his leg.

"Yes, Gideon likes to play the *patrone*."

"You think he patronizes you?" The thought had occurred to her.

Avner shrugged. "I have no illusions. Teachers and students don't stand on the same ground. But there are limits. Borders. I didn't expect him to tell you to leave me."

She looked over at him. "Not you. The country.

And what I said was all out of context. Gideon was just being cynical. And his unhappiness with Tsipi just gave that extra bite."

He met her gaze. "But that's the point. Why should he tell you these things? And why should you be so interested?"

She reddened. "I'm not interested in him *that* way, if that's what you mean."

Avner put his head back and closed his eyes. "No, it's not just the jealousy," he said, swallowing. "It's deeper."

She reached up and kissed his Adam's apple. From the balcony outside their room, she could hear Udi shouting directions for the climb up Mt. Sinai. "We need to be alone," she whispered. "It's spending all this time together and not really being together."

He lifted her hair and nuzzled her neck.

"I have an idea," she said. "Let's forget Mt. Sinai. We'll spend the afternoon together. Make love. And then see the monastery."

"And what will we tell the others?" She could feel him smiling.

"Anything you want. Or nothing at all." She turned to face him, wrapping her legs around his waist.

"We can't just not go." He kissed the inside

corners of her eyes. "We traveled three days to get here. We're part of a group."

"I don't *want* to be part of any group," she pleaded. "We'll make our own group, you and me. Isn't that what we're trying to do? Why you left your *moshav*? Why I'm staying on here?"

There was a knock at the door, and Udi's voice. "Okay, let's get moving."

"You don't understand," he said, smoothing her hair.

"No. *You're* the one who doesn't understand." She got up and walked into the bathroom. Garish turquoise tiles, like something out of an odd-lot warehouse, covered the walls. The fixtures were orange. She turned on the taps. Both ran cold.

When she came out, the room was empty. She put on a hat and stepped out onto the balcony.

"You're not climbing?" Udi said to her.

She glanced down. She'd forgotten to change into sneakers. She was about to go back inside when she noticed that Gideon too was in sandals.

"My arm still hurts, I don't think I will be able to climb today," she suddenly said, staring at the ground.

"Rebecca!" Avner took a step toward her.

She went on staring.

After a silence, Udi clapped his hands and shouted, "*Hevrah kadima!*" Group forward!

"So what do we do?" Gideon looked at her through slitted eyes. They were both leaning over the balcony. Below them, not far from wooden racks where white sheets were drying, three servants were crouched over a sheshbesh board.

"What do you suggest?" Her hand trembled on the wooden railing. "You're the one who's been here before."

"We could visit the past residents in the skull room. We could see a mosaic of the transfiguration of Christ. Highly educational." He paused, smiling. "Or we can take Udi's keys and go out looking for some cigarettes."

She tossed her head. "Can I drive?"

He glanced at her sore arm. She turned her wrist and smiled.

"So just an excuse." He lifted his eyebrows.

"What's yours?"

Eyebrows still lifted, he smiled. "I don't need one."

Rebecca shifted into gear and the jeep leaped forward. She laughed. "So where do I look for cigarettes? Is there a general store or something?"

"Let's head back where we came from. I saw some flat houses not far from where we saw the Bedouin."

After a couple of miles the gravel road became a rutted path. She found herself singing snatches of songs she hadn't sung in years.

When Gideon looked over at her and smiled, she said, "I haven't felt like this since I played hooky in high school. I never knew I was going to until I got there. Some days I couldn't go inside. I was sure I'd suffocate if I did."

He stretched an arm around the back of her seat.

"Those first moments I'd run, across the softball field and into the woods, scared shitless. But five minutes later, I'd feel this crazy high." She laughed again.

Gideon began to whistle.

"So why are we playing hooky together?" he suddenly asked. "I mean I know why *I* am. I wish Tsipi would just go off with Doron and be done with it. But she wants me there looking on, making sure nothing happens. A good little girl, Tsipi. There's nothing she's more afraid of than a bad conscience."

"Avner, too," she said, nodding.

"And you?"

She was aware of him looking at her. "I'm not afraid of a bad conscience," she said, lifting her chin.

"Seriously?"

"Seriously I asked *Avner* to play hooky with me."

She made a face. "I don't think he knows what the word means — in any language."

"That's why he's a good assistant. Also a good soldier. And probably one day a good husband."

"In other words you think he's limited, like Tsipi." Rebecca gripped the steering wheel tighter. This section of the ravine was strewn with large rocks washed down by the winter rains.

"I think he's extremely intelligent. Unlike Tsipi."

"That's not an answer," she said, realizing as she said it these were her exact words to Avner that morning.

"I keep answers for the classroom. Or did you forget we're playing hooky?"

She looked over at him. He was running his palm over his stubbly chin. "I never forget anything," she said. "Like you."

They started laughing.

Rebecca noticed the boulder too late. She swerved but the boulder had already thudded up and lodged under the vehicle's front end.

The jeep dragged to a halt.

Gideon saw the boys first. Rebecca only looked up when she heard Gideon say, "*Cigaria. Cigaret. Poof. Poof.*"

They had taken a break from building up the front

wheels with stones, and were drinking out of the built-in water tank that still contained an emergency supply.

The boys stopped about twenty feet away. Rebecca recognized the oversized sneakers.

"*Cigaria. Cigaret. Poof. Poof,*" Gideon repeated.

The boy with the sneakers approached and handed him a lighted cigarette.

"*Shukran.*" Gideon inhaled, and passed the cigarette to Rebecca. She took a drag and passed it back.

The boy watched, his eyes following the cigarette back and forth between them. Finally, he pointed to Gideon's wedding ring and gestured to Rebecca.

Gideon clicked his tongue no and winked at Rebecca.

The boy grinned.

Rebecca and Gideon smoked in the long shadow of the jeep with the sandal-footed boy, while his friend with the sneakers went to fetch a camel and rope. Rebecca didn't know the time because Gideon had handed over his digital watch. The boy with sneakers insisted the watch was for his uncle or cousin with the camel. No watch, no camel. In return, Gideon got his friend and a pack of cigarettes.

She could tell Gideon enjoyed the deal. Cigarette between his teeth, arm around her shoulder, he kept saying things like, "So hostage, what do we do with you if your friend doesn't return?" And when the boy didn't answer, or smile, or even accept the cigarette Gideon held out to him, Gideon said to her, "I think you make him nervous, Rebecca. All that skin. They're not used to it."

While Gideon was still negotiating with the boys, she'd checked for the gun she knew Udi had taken into the monastery. Now, watching the glum boy, she imagined a knife tied to his ankle. Or his friend not returning. Or returning, but with a bunch of Bedouin. She wished Gideon would remove his arm from her shoulder, but his hand wouldn't budge, not even when he began to build a castle from the splintery stones all around them. She watched him pile stone upon stone.

"What will they think if they get back from Mt. Sinai and find we're gone?" she finally blurted out.

Gideon gave her a sidelong smile.

"And what if the boy doesn't come back? Then what?"

"Relax." Gideon patted her shoulder with one hand as he reached for a stone with the other.

The ground in front of them was strewn with cigarette butts, but picked clean of stones. Now for his castle Gideon had to reach almost to the sandaled feet of their captive.

And then, finally, when the sun had sunk almost to the ridge, she spotted the boy, a black silhouette moving along like an overgrown slug. With a burst of relief, she jumped up and slapped the dust from her pants. But as she did so she became aware of something sharp poking into her. Reaching into her pocket, she came out with Tsipi's red stone.

She set it down carefully on the castle's peak. "There! How's that?"

Gideon laughed. "Perfect!"

But on closer view, she saw that the boy was perched on a scrawny grey mule, his sneakers practically dragging on the ground. Even the coiled rope around the animal's neck seemed too much of a burden.

She expected Gideon to be angry, or feel cheated. She did. But he just shook his head and laughed again.

"You have a strange sense of humor," she said.

Gideon got to his feet. "And what do you think I should do? Send back the mule, like the wrong food in a restaurant?"

Still with a cigarette between his teeth, Gideon tied the rope to the rear bumper. Then Rebecca put the engine in neutral, and while the boys beat the animal, Gideon gripped the grille and pushed. The jeep rolled free.

They all cheered, just like in the movies.

Gideon untied the rope and handed it back to the boy with the sneakers. "*Shukran.*"

The two boys stood, waiting.

Gideon dug into his pocket and pulled out some change.

The boys reached for the money, inspected each piece, looked at each other, and handed it all back. The boy with the sneakers then pointed to Gideon's gold ring.

Gideon clicked his tongue.

The boys didn't move.

He shook his finger. "No, no, no."

They continued to stare.

Finally Gideon shrugged, took Rebecca's arm, and led her to the jeep. He started the engine. Suddenly, a stone flew in the window, just missing his face. A second stone struck Rebecca's shoulder.

"Damn it!" she burst out, grabbing the pained flesh. "Why couldn't you just give them the lousy ring!"

Gideon reeled the jeep around and headed for the boys. They dropped the mule's rope and started running.

As the jeep overtook them, Rebecca tried to take

the wheel, but Gideon held tight. She closed her eyes and screamed. The thud sent her reeling against the door.

At first she didn't understand. As Gideon spun into reverse, she saw the boys staring out from behind an outcropping of rock.

Then she saw the mule on its side, its front feet tangled in the discarded rope.

Rebecca and Gideon climbed the stone staircase. A gong was calling the monks for evening prayers. She didn't see a single monk, not on the stairs, not on the balcony, not in the courtyard below. The only evidence of their existence seemed to be the iridescent white sheets no one had bothered to take in.

As the gong faded, Rebecca heard a distant guitar and Doron's love song.

"Damn fools," Gideon said, breaking the silence they had kept during the entire ride back.

She thought Gideon was referring to love. That it didn't exist. Couldn't. This was the code. The message he'd been trying to give her. She said nothing. She was beyond words, beyond feeling.

Outside Doron's room they halted. Rebecca stared at the ground and waited. "So our hooky day is over," Gideon finally said, his voice barely audible above the music.

She imagined him smiling. Suddenly, she looked up, she had to know for sure. But he had already turned and was walking away.

She watched until she couldn't see him any more.

For a moment she hesitated. Then she took a deep breath and entered the room.

Inside, it was pitch black except for a dull grey fringe around the window. Again she had the feeling of being in a box, only tonight she felt no fear, no desire to flee. Instead she stood with her head bowed, grateful for the dark, waiting for the song to be over.

Suddenly, behind her the door opened. Her first reaction was that it was Gideon. He'd changed his mind and come to join them. But turning, she recognized the monk who had welcomed them that morning, his gappy beard like barbed wire in the reflected balcony light.

Doron's voice swelled as he strummed the final chord.

When the last sound ceased, the monk put his finger to his lips and spoke.

"Shhhhh. Please. This is a monastery. You are guests here."

Then he walked out, closing the door firmly behind him.

In the silence afterward, Rebecca listened for Avner's deep, steady breathing, hoping it would lead her to him.

8.
LIKE A BRIDE ACROSS A THRESHOLD. . .

From the doorway, Rebecca looked back. The tile floor gleamed. A Yemenite shawl draped the orange-crate coffee table, and fresh anemones, their petals closed tight, filled the vase that Avner had bought the day they moved in. Humming along with the Hebrew song on the army station, she pulled the key from the lock, picked up the waiting pail of garbage, and listened for the door to click shut. The metal hinges of the pail's handle squeaked as she walked down the stairs. She was feeling good. All on her own, without Avner, she had prepared for Yom Kippur, washed the floors, decorated their flat with flowers.

Outside, the Jerusalem street was empty. Anyone who was going anywhere for dinner had already arrived, and yet dusk and *Kol Nidre* services were still a while off. At the garbage shed, she expertly kicked the asbestos siding, once, twice, to scatter the cats. She heard the soft, muffled padding of feet, but none of the clatter she had come to expect. Peeking inside, she discovered why. Every can was overflowing, and even the spaces between them were stuffed with holiday garbage. Taking aim from the doorway, she let the garbage fly. Unfortunately, she let her key fly as well.

At first she refused to believe the key was really lost. Her fingers traced a path over her scattered garbage, only occasionally poking beneath the surface. But before long she was flinging aside chicken carcasses and metal cans, sifting through huge handfuls of potato peelings, groping on her hands and knees. By the time she finished, she had plowed a path from the door to the cans. Her stomach was a small hard ball against her chest.

Outside the shed, picking eggshells off her jersey, she considered what to do. Avner was away for army reserve duty in Sinai for the month. His university friends were all home for the holidays. Everyone she had come over with had returned to the States in June. And she knew she had a better chance of finding her key in the garbage than she had of finding a locksmith tonight. Still not knowing what she was going to do, she walked back inside. At her front door she heard a high, shrill noise. She had left the radio on, and Galei Zahal, too, had shut down.

She took a few steps across the hall and listened. Mr Viorst, a Romanian engineer who clicked his heels whenever he said hello, was clapping his hands and shouting orders above the wails of his two-year old. She continued up to the third floor.

The first thing she noticed was the name plate on the door. Instead of the typical brass, copper or ceramic plate, there was only a yellowing slip of paper — Paulina Keller — in a faded European scrawl. In Rebecca's month here, she had never seen or heard the woman, only the chimes of her clock in the middle of the night and the crackles and beeps of her short-wave radio.

A light came from under the woman's door, but the radio was silent. She knocked.

"Yes. Who is it?" The voice was old, wary. Rebecca imagined the woman looking out at her through the one-way peephole that made everyone look mongoloid.

"You don't know me," she said in Hebrew. "My name is Rebecca. I live downstairs."

A bolt snapped, a key turned, and the door opened.

Paulina Keller, hair pulled back tight, yellow pinched eyes, extended her hand. "Nice to meet you," she said in English.

Rebecca looked at the formal, outstretched hand, then at her own hands, the fish-skin palms, the sludge under her fingernails. "I can't." She dangled her hands in front of her. "Look at me."

"The landlady lives with her daughter in Tel-Aviv," Rebecca explained. "And Avner left three days ago for *miluim*." She forced a smile. "You know, getting a tan on the Suez Canal. And. . . "

"And you're all alone."

There was a silence. Rebecca nodded.

Mrs Keller turned her eyes away.

Rebecca looked around the living room. From the chimes and the foreign broadcasts that had drifted down to their apartment, she had imagined a room covered in knickknacks and doilies, but it was plainer even than her own. Take away the enormous radio and the pendulum clock, and the only decoration left would be a scraggly philodendron reaching for the ceiling and a stack of *Ukelet* newspapers.

"You must wash up." Mrs Keller spoke a halting, exact English, the accent not quite German.

Rebecca followed the old woman into the bathroom. It was spare and white and worn like the rest of the flat, without even a shower curtain to enclose the depression in the floor where the drain

was, or a real medicine cabinet — just a white wooden
box with a red *Magen David* tacked to the wall.

When Rebecca turned on the sink tap, Mrs Keller
shook her head. "Take a shower, please, for the holiday."

Rebecca looked down. Her pants clung and her
cuffs sagged. She smelled like bad pickles. "I don't
know how you held out your hand to me."

"I can give you a dress, too. That is, if you want."

A half hour later Rebecca, wearing a loose, stretchy
brown dress and a pair of flesh-colored *gatkes*, was
seated across the table from the old woman. "You're
very kind," Rebecca said.

Paulina Keller shrugged. "I'm sorry I don't have a
better meal to offer you." She had spread out cheese,
olives, bread, a typical Israeli supper, but not a holiday dinner, and surely not one for Erev Yom Kippur. "Do you fast?"

"I never did before, but I thought maybe this year
I would. Avner does."

"Yes, Yemenites are very traditional. Did you have
one of those big weddings and — "

"We're not married," Rebecca interrupted. "We
just lied to get the flat." She waited. One thing to lie
to her landlord, another to an old woman whose
underpants she was wearing.

She offered Rebecca some olives. "My daughter tells me this is the *moda* nowadays. 'Trying it out,' they call it, no?"

"You have children?" Rebecca was surprised — and eager to change the subject. She had assumed that Paulina Keller had never married.

"One daughter."

Rebecca waited, but the old woman didn't continue.

"The olives are very good," Rebecca said finally.

Later in the evening, Rebecca and Mrs Keller sat facing each other in the living room. The enormous old radio was on a formica cart in front of the window, just where Rebecca would have expected to see a television set in most Israeli homes. Even though the radio was off, she couldn't help looking at it, perhaps because there was nothing else to look at.

"How many languages do you speak?" Rebecca asked, grasping for something to say.

Mrs Keller shrugged. "Five. Six."

"I only have room in my head for two languages." Rebecca tapped her temple, Israeli-style. "I used to know French, but when I learned my Hebrew, I lost it."

"Ah. This is because Hebrew doesn't work the way a language should." She folded her arms under her bosom. "Three months in Paris and I spoke wonderful French. Twenty-five years here and I still break my teeth."

"Did you end up in Paris after the war?"

She pointed her chin at Rebecca. "You Americans think nobody knew what a train was before Auschwitz. From my university in Budapest I went to study for a year at the Sorbonne. This is 1927. Hitler was still painting houses."

"And my great-grandfather was still a peddler," Rebecca said, smiling.

"And Lindbergh just flew across the Atlantic." Mrs Keller fastened her eyes on Rebecca. "I was coming home from classes. It was spring. Also early evening. And there were birds in the trees. Hundreds. Thousands. You couldn't hear the trolleys. And people? The sidewalks were full of them, and every one with the head back like this." Mrs Keller lolled back her head and let her jaw drop.

Rebecca leaned forward.

"I thought it was the birds they were looking at. Until someone shouted. '*Voyez. Voyez. Lindbergh est arrivé.*' And I saw it, too, no bigger than all the other birds that night." She paused. "We went crazy, all of us, hugging and kissing." Mrs Keller ended with her eyes closed.

Rebecca stared. She wanted to say something, but

she didn't know what.

The old woman opened her eyes. "Did you ever see birds like that? I never did again."

Rebecca shook her head. "But in California we have birds that chirp only at night."

"*Fantasti*. Because of the lights?"

"Because it's California." Rebecca laughed. "Everything goes in reverse in California."

"Everything?"

"The people, for instance. I have an aunt. She looks my age and she must be. . ." Rebecca fingered the air.

". . . my age?"

"It's not right. Not natural."

Mrs Keller's yellow eyes glinted. "You think old people should look old."

"I think life should go in the right direction," Rebecca said, nodding. "That's what I've grown to love about Israel. There's a rhythm and everyone follows it. Like tonight. There's not a car out there."

Together they listened. Not a motor or radio or telephone in all the neighborhood.

"And you don't think this rhythm of yours is also a little 'not right'? 'Unnatural'? After all, this is why you must be up here, and not down there." Mrs Keller rapped the floor with her thick, black heel.

"What happened was my own fault."

"Why?"

"I shouldn't have lost my key. I should have been more careful."

Mrs Keller smiled, just the slightest. "My grandfather used to say, 'Even God has to sneeze once in a while.'"

From the moment Mrs Keller gave Rebecca her dress to change into, Rebecca knew she'd be spending the night with the old woman. After making up her bed on the sofa with starched white sheets, Rebecca leaned out the window as far as she could. Her lights downstairs were on and she could just make out Avner's old sandal wedged into their broken second-floor window to keep it from slamming shut.

As hard as Rebecca tried, she couldn't fall asleep. The clock chimed. The sheets scratched. And she missed Avner. Even Mrs Keller's narrow sofa seemed too big. Her leg kept groping for something to wrap around.

Just after three, she knew by the chimes, she heard a car shift gears and come to a halt outside. She listened. The unmistakable scrape of boots on pavement. Avner. Laughing, she rushed to the window. She was just in time to see a man in fatigues jump into the passenger seat of a white army car and wave out the window. Looking up, Rebecca saw a woman in the lighted window of the opposite apartment block. The woman's hair was loose, her shoulders bare, and she was waving back.

Mrs Keller unwrapped the tiny packets of cheese and olives and bread she had wrapped up after dinner and offered Rebecca a plate.

Rebecca gestured she was fasting. She realized that this was probably all the food the woman had in the house.

"The sofa was fine?"

"Fine. Really fine."

"My daughter used to tell me that it smelled like a donkey. From the stuffing, I guess."

"I didn't smell anything."

"Of course, that was over twenty years ago. She used to come home on Shabbat from Youth Aliya."

Rebecca knew that in the early days children of single refugee mothers who had to go out to work often lived away in youth camps. "It must have been hard having your daughter live away from you," she said.

Mrs Keller shrugged. "After the first year Vera could have come back if she wanted. But she didn't want."

Nodding, Rebecca looked around. The room

seemed even emptier in daylight than it had at night.

"By then it didn't matter so much anyway. I was used to the space between us. The war did that. The ones who didn't come back left a space in the family. In the beginning you try to fill it up. Always a new toy, a new coat, a new country. Then one day you stop." She cut a slice of bread. "And you?"

"Me what?" Rebecca didn't understand the connection.

"You're not used to being alone. It can't be easy."

"I used to be better at it." Rebecca smiled. "But these last three days, whenever I hear boots, or see an army car, I imagine it's Avner." She nudged the bread crumbs with her finger. "Even last night. There was an army car pulled up outside. It must have been the only car in Jerusalem."

Mrs Keller looked up, startled.

"I thought Avner got a lift back. That maybe he didn't really care about it being Yom Kippur. But the car was picking someone up over there." Rebecca tipped her chin. Mrs Keller followed the motion with her eyes. "I saw a woman waving from the third-floor window."

Turning back to Rebecca, Mrs Keller said, "This is the first time Avner leaves you to go to the army?"

"He was supposed to go at the beginning of the summer, just after I decided to stay on, but he didn't want to leave me. So he told his officer he had a toothache."

"And he couldn't make such a reason again?" Mrs Keller laughed.

"This time I wouldn't let him."

When Mrs Keller raised her brows, Rebecca added, "The army is so much part of the life here."

"Ah. The rhythm."

Rebecca hesitated. She sensed she was being laughed at. "I also wanted to prove that I could manage on my own. That I was the same as everyone else here."

"If you were the same as everyone else you'd let him stay home with a make-believe toothache."

Though this Yom Kippur fell in October, there wasn't a breath of air in the apartment. Mrs Keller's bun of hair sagged. Sweat filled the loose, stretchy folds of Rebecca's borrowed dress.

Rebecca asked the question that had been going through her head all morning. "Do you wish you'd stayed in Paris?" It had dawned on her that if she and Mrs Keller had made different choices, small choices in retrospect, they both could have ended up in Paris, meeting there perhaps as they were meeting here.

Mrs Keller looked up, squinting into the sunlight.

"I think I know what you meant about that day with the birds," Rebecca continued. "One day this winter I went for a walk in the wadi on the old border, near the railroad tracks." She began to speak faster. "The crumbling terraces look like bleachers in an enormous amphitheater. When I started down, I couldn't even see the bottom. Before long I was running and leaping down the broken terraces. At the bottom, on the railroad tracks, I passed two Arab workmen. Maybe I should have been afraid, but I wasn't. Just the opposite. I wished I had a way to let them know, but all I could do was nod."

"But you didn't stay because of the wadi or the workmen. You stayed because of the boy."

Rebecca caught her lip. "That's not what I tell people. My parents."

"When I was young, we didn't need so much the excuses. I returned to Budapest because I was in love."

The clock sounded two dull chimes.

"That's when we got the clock. My husband's grandmother gave it to us for the engagement."

Rebecca got up and walked to the window. She leaned against the sill, head cradled in her arms. The afternoon heat had chased everyone inside except for some children playing leapfrog in the street.

"Is that the woman you saw?"

Rebecca started. She hadn't felt Mrs Keller come up behind her. Shading her eyes against the sun, she searched for the window. The glare made the building look much further away, and the woman, so clear the night before, was now just a blur of hair. Rebecca nodded. She was about to say that the woman looked as if she'd been there all night, when she heard a crack of static. Turning around, Rebecca saw the old woman crouched over her radio.

". . . reports of a clash between Israeli and Egyptian forces on the Suez Canal . . ." said the BBC announcer in the same flat tone in which he announced the weather.

Rebecca looked up at the clock. Two minutes after two. She was still looking at it when the sirens went off.

On their way down to the shelter, they bumped into Mr Viorst, baby flung over his shoulder, bag of potato chips in one hand, transistor in the other. "It's nothing," he said, clicking his heels.

The shelter was stuffed with broken stoves and refrigerators and Mr Viorst's wooden packing crates, but nobody seemed to mind. "Nonsense," they said to each other, spilling out into the entry and onto the front steps. When Rebecca looked up at the sky, an old woman in a kerchief giggled, "Not here." Then, stretching her arms out at her side and flapping them like a dotty bird, she added, "In Suez!"

Turning back to Mrs Keller, Rebecca asked, "Is this a war?"

"You expected something else?"

By three o'clock it seemed more like a war, but still not what Rebecca had expected. Half the mobilization passwords on the radio sounded like lipsticks, the other half song titles. Most of the army reservists looked like Mr Viorst, bald and paunchy, uniform too tight, boots missing, with plastic bags instead of rucksacks trailing from their arms.

Back upstairs after the all-clear signal, Rebecca looked for the woman in the window, but her metal blinds were shut tight. "Probably gone to her mother's," Mrs Keller told her. This, too, surprised Rebecca. She wouldn't have expected a married woman to run home to her mother. But as the afternoon wore on she realized that as many cars were coming for mothers and children as for soldiers.

At four o'clock Mrs Keller told Rebecca that they should fill some containers in case the water was cut off. Since the old woman had only two pots and no bathtub, Rebecca scrubbed a wash pail for her and filled that with water, too. All this time they listened to the news, flipping back and forth between Kol Israel and the BBC. The BBC told of a reported Egyptian crossing of the canal, Kol Israel only of a surprise attack on two fronts.

Rebecca finally blurted out what she'd been thinking ever since the sirens went off. "Avner's not even supposed to be there on the canal. If only I made him go in June. Or if I let him stay home with a toothache."

They were standing in the kitchen. The pots were on the counter, the pail on the floor.

"You should eat something," Mrs Keller said.

"It's all like a bad joke."

"Really. You must eat." She opened the refrigerator and took out the tiny packets of food.

"Even your knowing is crazy. Here Golda Meir says it's a surprise attack and you knew. I know you did."

Mrs Keller unwrapped the cheese.

"It was the car in the middle of the night, wasn't it? The woman in the window."

"We have a joke. Some men are like litmus paper for border troubles." She looked at Rebecca. "He's one of them. His wife says every time he's called up, you read something in the paper the next morning."

"But you turned on the radio at the exact moment. It doesn't make sense." Rebecca hit the counter. Water sloshed in the pot.

"Maybe you expect life to make too much sense."

Rebecca caught the hard angry edge to the woman's voice. "I'm sorry. I was never in a war before." She said it seriously, so seriously that both of them started laughing. "I feel I should be doing something, but I don't know what. Tell me. What do people do in a war?"

Mrs Keller held out a slice of cheese on a piece of bread. "They wait."

In the street two girl soldiers slapped baby-blue paint on car headlights. Blackout curtains began to appear in living room windows. Instead of the usual attached balconies, the cheap 1950s flats in this part of Jerusalem had glass doors opening into nowhere and wrought-iron safety gates. So while all the other windows could be blacked out by a flick of a cord, these door-windows had to be covered by hand.

Mrs Keller gave Rebecca a heavy black cloth in the shape of a door, and she tacked it onto the wooden rim. She tried to use the same holes that were already there, from '67 she supposed. By the time she had finished, she could barely see Mrs Keller mov-

ing across the room to the front door. All the time
she had been putting up the curtain, she had heard
a banging, but it had been indistinguishable from
all the other street noises. Horns. Whistles. Shouts.
Radios. Now she realized that the banging was coming from the downstairs hallway.

Flying out the door and down the stairs, all Rebecca could think was, "It's too early to know. Too
early to know." Still, when she saw black boots in
front of her door, she froze. It hadn't occurred to her
that they'd never come here, to their apartment, but
to Avner's parents' *moshav*.

"Lady, you got to cover your window."

Looking up, Rebecca saw a grey-haired man, flash-
light in one hand, whistle around his neck.

"I'm locked out," she said, walking down the last
few steps. "I can't get in."

Within minutes, the lock was smashed and her
door wide open.

From outside, she stared in. The floor gleamed.
The shawl covered the crate table. And the bouquet
of anemones, their red and purple buds swollen to
the size of golfballs, filled the pitcher.

She smiled and stepped inside, like a bride crossing a threshold.

9.

AT THE OLD BORDER

The locksmith had been mobilized, she found out the next morning, as had the owner of the electrical shop and the man who fixed motor scooters in a shack behind the movie house. As a last resort, she stopped in at the neighborhood candy store that was not only open, but busy. All the children, it seemed, had been packed off with pockets of change. "He'll grow up soon enough," one mother chided another who was telling her son to choose between a chocolate bar and a swirled lolly. The owner, a chalky-faced Polish woman, told Rebecca to try Glickstein, a pensioner who repaired appliances in his home.

"Poor unfortunate," Glickstein said to Rebecca after she had explained that she had locked herself out. He was short and shirtless, with a belly that hung over his pants. "All alone yet. Who can keep his head in times like these? Did you hear? Moshe Dayan shot himself last night after his broadcast. During *Ironside*. And eighteen women were raped and butchered on the Golan Heights. The newspapers? The only thing the Israeli newspapers are good for is wiping your bottom."

Without bothering to put on a shirt, he grabbed a fistful of tools and followed her out. When she said she probably needed a new lock, that it was beyond repair, he said, "Nonsense. No such thing. Everyone knows a shopkeeper will tell you anything to sell you his junk."

Before he set to work, he stepped into her living room and looked around. "Ah, your husband's a man of feeling," he said, nodding at a shelf of Hebrew poetry.

She smiled.

"But he shouldn't have left you alone. Where's his family? Call-up or no call-up, a man has a duty. It's written in the Bible." And then he said something in flowery Hebrew she didn't understand.

"I'm fine alone," she said, swallowing. "And anyway he wasn't called up. He was already on reserve duty."

"Oh? Where?"

"The Canal."

A moment of silence, and then he set to work on

the lock, picking and poking and hammering.

She asked him if he wanted coffee; he only clicked his tongue and grunted. She questioned him about Moshe Dayan and the girls on the Golan, but he said, "Rumors. Gossip. Don't believe a word of it."

A half hour later, he pushed himself up off his knees, flicked the door knob a few times, and said, "You see? Good as new. Just like I promised."

She thanked him and asked how much she owed.

"Nothing, nothing at all," he said, reaching out and patting her shoulder.

She persisted, but he remained firm. Suddenly, she was reminded of the children packed off to the candy store. She resolved that from now on, if anyone asked about Avner, where he was stationed, she would say, "Somewhere in Sinai" — just as the radio announcers did when they played songs dedicated to soldiers.

Waiting, she discovered, demanded all her energy and concentration, so that by nine o'clock in the evening she would fall into bed, the back of her knees aching, as if she had been washing floors all day. After the first days, everyone was talking postcards. At the grocer's, in the bank, on the bus. Did you? Didn't you? When? And then those who had heard would tell those who hadn't that it really didn't matter. In the best of times the mail system was worth shit. "Send eight letters and you're lucky if nine aren't lost."

Looking out from behind the blanket she had tacked to her window frame, she would watch for the pensioner who had replaced their regular mailman. Spotting him, she would hurry out on the landing and listen. The lock on their mailbox was broken, so instead of using the letter slot, the mailman would swing open the little metal door. A few times she heard the squeak of hinges and rushed down, trembly and out of breath.

But all she found were blue airgrams from her parents sent before the war. That's what she noticed. Not the words, she barely glanced at them, but the date in the right-hand corner. Eight days before the war. Two days before. She wracked her brain trying to remember what she'd been doing, saying, wearing. What did she cook? Did she and Avner make love? How? Once she got a postcard, but it was from Mr Viorst, written in Romanian, deposited in her box by mistake.

Then there was the wait for the telephone. Not hers and Avner's, they didn't have one, but the Viorsts' across the hall. Avner had taken their number with him. The second day of the war, shortly after her lock was repaired, she heard the phone, and then the Viorsts' door open. In the hall she met Mrs Viorst who, no doubt reading her face, burst out: "America, your father." Rebecca had forgotten she had given him the Viorsts' number.

Yes, of course she was fine. The newspapers were stupid. No one here even bothered with them. Come home? Of course not. Her friend? Her friend was fine. Somewhere in Sinai. By the way, he didn't happen to hear that Moshe Dayan shot himself? No? Rumors, gossip, you couldn't believe a word of it.

In the evenings she would go upstairs for an hour or so and listen with Mrs Keller to the foreign broadcasts on the enormous old radio in front of the black-curtained window. Neither of them spoke much. Rebecca became accustomed to the living room, even began to like its bareness. In her mind it became one with the old woman's silence. She had tried to return the brown knit dress, placing it, washed and folded, on top of a basket of food she left on Mrs Keller's doorstep. But that evening Mrs Keller came downstairs and held out the dress. "Please," she said, nothing more, neither about the dress nor the food.

About a week after the war started, Rebecca stopped going out, except in the morning for milk and bread, and sometimes flowers that the grocer kept in a bucket next to the register. She sat for hours on her sofa, which was really a straw mattress on a metal frame covered with a cloth, stared at the flowers, and thought about spaces. Her living room. The only space she felt to be her own since she arrived here. Mrs Keller's daughter. *People who die leave spaces in a family.* And how about inner spaces? Spaces in the heart or gut or soul? That's what she felt growing inside her these past days: a space more alive than anything she had ever known, fed by all this waiting. Just the opposite of the emptiness she had come here with: a void begging to be filled — with men, houses, exotic landscapes.

On the tenth day of the war, a little after nine, she saw the first death notice. She had just left the grocery, milk and bread and flowers in hand, when she saw people bunched up in front of the Hungarian bakery. The lights were off, and a black-bordered notice was gummed to the glass door. Everyone was talking at once. "They finally came around last night . . . They say Moshe Dayan himself made calls . . . Poor thing was going to America to study, even had his ticket . . . It's wrong waiting so long . . . They say it's the rabbinate. They want proof. What proof is there if nothing's left . . ."

Rebecca ran back to her apartment. All day she sat.

She didn't listen for the mail or the telephone or the scrape of boots. Around five, she got up, changed into Mrs Keller's dress and took a last look around. Then she closed the door gently behind her.

At the station, the Haifa bus was waiting, half empty, radio blaring, the driver and another old man arguing about whether the Americans would force a cease fire now that Israel was winning.

For most of the ride she sat alone, staring out the window. Coming down out of the mountains, the coastal plain stretched dry and parched as far as she could see, cotton bushes without cotton, mown fields strewn with straw. She had never known there could be so many shades of brown.

At some point a bosomy Moroccan woman with greying braids sat down next to her, a plastic bag of fruit on her lap. She offered Rebecca some dates and asked her if she was a social worker.

"Oh, you mean the dress," Rebecca said, glancing down.

The woman shrugged. "Maybe, but more the eyes. Hot and cold together." Then, patting Rebecca's leg, she added, "It's okay. I myself have nothing against social workers. They do the best they can."

Rebecca recognized the turn-off and pulled the

cord. The entire ride she had been imagining green, but the orange grove was more grey than green, an opaque rippling that stretched to the horizon. As she stepped off the bus she was hit by a dusty end-of-the-summer smell. She started walking. At the sandy shoulder where Avner had set down his suitcase, she willed herself to remember that other walk.

But she couldn't. Even here, now, it remained a blur, bits and pieces out of order.

All day it had been like that. Each time she had tried to gather together moments, fixing in her mind the details of touch and taste and smell that would give them weight and mass, they broke apart and scattered. Like drops of mercury that once free don't like to be touched. Until even Avner's face eluded her. If she saw his mouth, she couldn't see his eyes. And if she saw his eyes, it was on a day they had looked at her in pain.

She walked faster. In the moonlight the grove began to resemble a dwarf forest. A truck passed, its blue light sweeping over her. No beeps. No catcalls.

From the outskirts, the *moshav* looked dark, sleepy, its string of bungalows almost pretty. A hen pecked at her heels. "Leave me!" She kicked out, but the hen kept coming back. Maybe it was hungry. Maybe it was crazy. They said that because of the blackout many of the hens had stopped laying eggs.

What did light have to do with laying eggs? Fear?

She was running now, her eyes on the bend in the road. Please, please, please. It was a rhythm in her chest.

And then she heard it. A high-pitched noise. A woman's noise. Coming out of nowhere, it seemed, squeezing the air from her lungs, the last traces of hope from her heart. Lights and cars, people, these were what she had dreaded. But it was the noise of women that told her Avner was dead.

When the women finally came into view, swarms of them, inside the house and out, she thought of a wedding, a macabre wedding where the women go barefoot and beat their breasts and wail.

She couldn't go inside. She couldn't listen.

Running faster, she searched the blackness for the old barbed-wire border Avner had pointed out. But she could see nothing, no separation even between earth and sky. Still, she knew it was there. She could feel it pulling her, like a magnet, like a kiss. When the road ended, she pushed on into the scrubby underbrush. Prickers grabbed at her skin and dress. She fought back, squatting and flailing, wishing herself naked, wishing herself free. But it was no use. The scrub was too dense, too ruthless. The prickers reattached themselves faster than she could pull them off. Finally, she just crouched in her prisoner's squat, subdued but dry-eyed, looking around. For all her lashing out, she had put hardly any distance between herself and the road — and none at all between herself and the women. If anything she heard them with a clarity that had been missing before. Their pain. Her pain. As separate as their lives. Hers was silent, hard even, the way that space inside her was silent and hard. And yet alive.

Finally, she stood up. There was no place to run to. Nothing left to wait for. It was time to begin the journey back.